Keeping it family

Mai Roma

Copyright © 2021 Mai Roma

All rights reserved.

ISBN: 9798502615754

KEEPING IT IN THE FAMILY

CONTENTS

	Acknowledgments	ii
1	New Beginnings	Pg 2
2	Goodbye	Pg 12
3	Keep moving forward	Pg 19
4	Work	Pg 27
5	Trouble	Pg 34
6	Lips	Pg 50
7	This is wrong	Pg 63
8	I'm sorry	Pg 71
9	Why not	Pg 80
10	Finally	Pg 86
11	What are you doing?	Pg 96
12	Hold on	Pg 105
13	I don't know why you say goodbye	Pg 113

ACKNOWLEDGMENTS

This is the first real book I publish and it came to life because of my need to create my own story and characters I could control because TV shows kill all the characters I like or my favorite shows are all cancelled.

I want to thank my mum for always supporting me, my family and friends.

I also want to thank Danielle Renée Larkin and germancreative from fiver for helping me out.

And last but definitely not least, you. Whoever is reading this book is amazing. I really enjoyed writing this story so I hope you enjoy reading it.

I'm sure it's not a bestseller but for anyone to be reading this is a dream come true for me; so, thank you, and I won't bug you anymore so you can go on and start reading the book.

1 NEW BEGINNINGS

Everyone watched as the hundreds of nervous, excited, and well-dressed police officers walked down the aisle of the Madison Square Garden that had been habilitated to hold the police academy graduation ceremony. The first female police commissioner, Claudia Benzinni, sitting beside her husband, retired detective Richard Benzinni, watched proudly as the new recruits walked down the aisle preparing to go on that stage and become official New York City police officers. Both looked especially proud when one specific name was called out of the loudspeakers.

"Allison Benzinni," A loud audience clap was heard, especially loud compared to the rest of the claps the other recruits had received, but that wasn't because of her being the commissioner's daughter, it was because of the large family that was in the audience cheering her on.

Jackson Benzinni, his wife Mindy, both doctors at Mayflower West hospital, and their two boys Jamie and Peter. Sitting beside them Ellie Benzinni, New York City detective and her ten-year-old daughter Olivia and just a row behind Parker Benzinni, New York City Police Sargent, his wife Eve, an attorney at one of the most prestigious law firms in the city, their seven-year-old daughter and four-year-old twins all cheered loudly as Allison, the youngest daughter of Claudia and Richard Benzinni became an official police officer.

After the ceremony, they all went to have lunch at their childhood home, where they would usually have a family lunch or dinner a few times a month.

"So, the 31st precinct, Allison, are you excited?" Richard looked at his youngest daughter, who sat right to his side on the table. She seemed happy yet nervous at the same time.

"I'm not too keen on Parker being my sergeant, but I hope he'll at least give me a good training officer." She glanced at her brother, who was right in front of her feeding Maia, his youngest twin daughter, what was left on her plate.

"Well, I'm looking forward to being the boss of my little sister," Parker laughed, passing the mash potatoes to her eldest daughter.

"Aunt Ali, I thought you said we should never let a boy be our boss." The little girl, who looked just like her dad yet surprisingly more beautiful, looked at her aunt, asking for an explanation.

"And you shouldn't, Alex, not in your day-to-day but at work you have to listen to your boss no matter if he is a boy or a girl." Her niece looked at her with a funny face, not understanding. "It's like at school you have to listen to your teacher no matter if he's a boy or a girl."

"Alex never listens to her teachers no matter if they are boys or girls," Parker smiled, kissing his daughter's head with love. He truly was the best dad in the world.

Allison had looked up to her siblings all her life. Jackson was an amazing surgeon, truly great, and Ellie and Parker, thirty-seven-year-old twins, had always paved the way for Allison, who had come as a surprise to the family nine years after the twins had been born.

The Benzinni family was united, they were a strong, loving family who always had each other's back. Of course, they fought, especially about cases they were all involved in, but they were one of the most loving and caring families you would ever meet.

The lunch was quick yet entertaining. Soon enough, Claudia had to get back to her office, and everyone else had to go back to work. They kissed their kids, who would stay home with grandpa, and soon enough, Parker and Allison were on the way to their precinct.

Allison felt incredibly proud of herself when she thought about the fact that she was finally going to work. Well, she was only going to meet her training officer that day, but that was as good as any other day at work for her.

"You're going to love me when you see who I paired you up with."

They arrived at the precinct, and you could just see there was so much new blood. All the happy and nervous faces looked at the lists where they would find who they would work with until further notice.

Parker barely had any time to wish his sister good luck before she was running inside to see who her brother had chosen for her to start her new life. She went in running, and she soon realized that had been a mistake, she was on the floor after having bumped with someone.

"Officer, please pull yourself together," She could've recognized that voice anywhere.

"Mom… I mean, Ma'am… What are you doing here?" Allison was crossing her fingers as hard as she could while recomposing herself for her Mom not to be there to check up on her.

"Officer Benzinni, on the day of graduation, I always tour around the precincts making sure everything, and everyone is on point."

"Yes, of course, in that case, excuse me, Ma'am, I'm going to go and check who Sergeant Benzinni chose for me," She saluted her mother in the formal style and went to where the papers were hanging.

She was grateful her name started with 'B,' so she quickly found her name. She placed her finger on it and traced it looking for the name that was written right across from hers. Charlotte Reigns. A girl. Parker had given her a girl. She looked around, looking for her brother, and once she found him, she quickly made her way over to him.

"You paired me with a girl?" she hissed at him angrily, making sure no one heard her.

"You're welcome, I thought you would be excited to be paired with a girl, especially one like Charlotte Reigns?"

Charlotte Reigns was the best there was. She was the youngest officer to graduate from her class in the academy, she had been on the police force since she was 18, had amazing records, and aced all her exams. It hadn't even been his idea, Ellie had helped him make the pair.

"You know paired female officers never get any respect around this city, Parker."

"Ellie was the one who chose her Ali. She's a great cop, and she's been paired with female officers before and never had any problems. Make sure you're not the first to have problems with her, she's a very liked person around this city."

Allison grunted at her brother before turning around and heading to the lounge where she knew the training officers were. It was easy to find hers, she was the only woman there.

"Officer Reigns," She smiled as she approached her. When the girl turned around, Allison was shocked.

Charlotte Reigns was young, really young. Allison couldn't be much older than her, and Charlotte was beautiful. Yes, her short blond hair was in a bun, and she was wearing her uniform, but with beautiful brown eyes, she was an enigma. Allison was shocked, to say the least.

"You must be Allison Benzinni, right?"

"Yes, that's me," she could barely talk. She definitely didn't expect that.

"Great," she was so cheerful. "Okay, so first thing first, let's get out of here, so all these men stop eyeing you up and down" she looked back at her fellow police officers, and they threw their hands in the air like if they were innocent.

They went outside of the precinct and got into a car. It was a very elegant black car which she later found out belonged to Charlotte.

"So first of all, I know who you are" she turned to look at Allison as they hit a red light. "And I don't care, I'm going to treat you like I treat every other officer I have had the pleasure to train. I won't treat you as an inferior if you don't earn it. In my eyes, you are just like me, you are my partner, and I am your partner. Not your training officer."

"Can I ask you how old you are?" The second that came out of her mouth, she regretted it instantly. "I'm so sorry, that is so rude."

"I'm twenty-three."

"What? You can't be twenty-three and a training officer, you can't be a cop in New York until you're like twenty-one."

"I starting working as a Police Officer in Rhode Island when I turned eighteen years old, worked there for nearly four years, and transferred into the NYPD last year."

"Oh okay, that makes sense" Allison was confused, she was meant to see her training officer as a mentor, as someone who would take care of her, but she suddenly felt this sense of protection over this girl who was four years younger than her. When she was twenty-three, she was coming home half drunk from college parties all day.

"Can I continue with my speech now?" She laughed, and Allison couldn't help but laugh with her.

"Yes, of course."

"Okay, so, as I was saying, you are my partner, and as you probably can tell, we're both female cops. We are two of 17% of female officers in the NYPD, we are a two female partnership which is even less normal, so we have to prove ourselves more than any other male officer would have to. We can't make mistakes or get tired while chasing a subject or let someone we are trying to arrest push us to the floor because when we get back to the precinct, what they will probably say to us is that we are too weak to be out in the streets alone without any male officers to back us up, so I'm not letting that happen to us okay?"

"Understood. I promise I won't let you down."

"I know you won't." They drove for a while and talked about their lives until the car stopped, they were near Hudson River, and a restaurant with neon lights called Allison's attention. "This is my favorite spot to eat in this whole city, it's kind of far away, but the hamburgers are incredible. I'll let you pay, don't worry," She smiled and got out of the car.

Allison followed her inside, and soon enough, the smell of cooked meat filled her nostrils. It smelled incredible, much better than when she tried to cook at family meals.

After Charlotte had introduced her to the waiters, who she clearly knew well, they sat down in a booth and waited for the food Charlotte had ordered for the both of them.

"So, were you pressured into joining the job?"

"What?"

"I mean, your dad was one of the best detectives in this city, your Mom is the police commissioner, and you have two older siblings also working the job, so I'm just wondering if you're in this because you were pressured by your family to follow in their footsteps or you actually wanted to join."

Allison could see that she was genuinely interested in knowing, so she didn't take it the wrong way and answered her.

"I wasn't pressured, I mean, nearly all my family has been in the force, but I could have chosen something else. My eldest brother Jackson is a doctor, and that was never a problem. My parents would've understood if I had decided to do something else, but it didn't really feel right to be anything else other than a police officer."

"And your brother being our sergeant, is it going to be a problem?"

"No, definitely not. I mean, Parker and I get along okay, he'll probably play the protective older brother card if something goes wrong, but it won't interfere, I promise."

"I like you, Benzinni, I'm really liking you, so make sure you don't screw this partnership up doing some stupid superhero stunt on me on the first day."

"I'll listen to you all the time. I'm here with you to learn to be the best cop I can be"

She seemed satisfied with the answer because after eating, they went back to the precinct and showed Allison around, introduced her to some co-workers, and taught her how to use everything.

When they were about to leave and were changing in the locker rooms, Allison got the courage to ask her what she had been wanting to ask the whole day.

"Hey, I know we have to be up and working early tomorrow, but would you like to grab a drink, like off work, and talk about something other than my motives to be a police officer and my family" She put her sweater on trying to avoid eye contact for a few seconds while waiting for an answer. She didn't really know why she had asked that, she just felt like knowing her in a personal manner before starting to work together for months.

"I think that would be a great idea, Benzinni,"

"Allison, I mean, we're off work. You can call me Allison or Ali. Everyone calls me Ali," She nervously smiled.

"In that case, Ali, you can call me Charlie, no one really calls me Charlotte."

They left the precinct and headed to a nearby bar. They were having fun, Allison was laughing a bit too much at Charlotte's horrible jokes, but they seemed to have hit it off. Ali was sure that they would be great partners. What she couldn't have seen coming was what was about to go through the radio that Charlie always had connected.

"10-71 requesting back up at 135th street, north entrance St. Nicholas Park. Multiple shooters." They heard a lot of gunfire followed by an officer in clear distress. "Officer down, I repeat Officer down. Sergeant Benzinni is down. WE NEED HELP!"

Charlie looked up at Allison, whose eyes had filled up with tears.

"Allison, it's five minutes away from here, we can get there," she quickly held her hand and squeezed it. "He'll be okay." She grabbed her radio as she put a ten-dollar bill on the table.

"10-10 This is Off Duty Officer Reigns and Off Duty Officer Benzinni responding. We are two minutes out" They ran as fast as they could, Charlie kept looking back at Allison, making sure she didn't fall back. She was trying to think what to do, it was her brother, she hasn't even had a day at work, Allison didn't even have a gun on her.

They saw Parker lying on the floor as soon as they reached the park entrance, his partner was holding pressure on his chest. He looked pale, he didn't look okay. Allison ran to her brother, making sure he stayed awake.

"Don't you dare leave me, Parker, I swear," she tried to hold back her tears, she didn't want to make it worse. "Wake up, don't fall asleep, Parker, please."

"11-41 Where is that ambulance?" Charlie radioed again and then crouched down to Allison's level, took her hands, and placed them on top of Parker's chest. "Allison, you need to hold pressure. I need to go after the shooters, Officer Harrelson, back me up."

Allison did as she was told as the two officers went into the park.

"Parker, please don't die, please, please, please," She begged, looking around for the ambulance.

"Ali, I need you…."

"No, no goodbye speeches, you need to save your strength."

"Allison, tell Eve she's strong and make sure the girls know their dad was a good man, and you have to teach them to be good, Ali promise me."

"I promise," She cried, trying to hold as much pressure as she could.

"And tell Ellie she couldn't do anything, she was always the better twin, she…" he started coughing up blood, and Allison started to panic.

"WHERE THE HELL IS THAT AMBULANCE?"

Dozens of police cars started to arrive, some went into the park the same way Charlie had gone, and some started moving things around, setting up tapes, and separating possible witnesses. Allison couldn't help but think that was going to be the last time she was going to see her brother alive.

"You hold on, Parker, I'm not telling your girls they don't have a father anymore. You hold on!"

2 GOODBYE

Allison saw Ellie arrive at the scene minutes after the ambulance had. She was shaking, her hands were trembling, she could see on her face she didn't know what was happening, what to expect. She saw how she looked around trying to find a familiar face but couldn't see anything with the mass of police officers and paramedics that swarmed the area. She finally saw her and looked at her blood-filled hands hugging Charlie. Allison was crying, she was crying too much and that made Ellie extremely anxious.

"Allison, what? What happened? Is he?" Ellie grabbed her sister's arm, making her let go of the hug she was trying to take refuge in.

"He… he…Ellie… he" She tried, but she couldn't talk.

"He's critical," Charlie took over, seeing how Allison was too overcome to talk. "He has two gunshot wounds in the upper left side of his chest. The medics are working on him now."

"Was he conscious? Was he breathing?" Ellie kept on talking to her sister, which made her more distraught and she found she couldn't talk. Ellie's eyes grew wide, looking fearful, and she shook Allison, yelling "ALLISON TALK TO ME"

"He was talking, and then he wasn't Ellie. I tried… I started CPR, but the ambulance got here just a few seconds later, they pushed me away," Charlie placed her hand on her back, trying to give her some sort of comfort.

Ellie ran to where they were treating her brother, she saw him lying on the floor, no one was doing CPR but they where trying to stop his bleeding which meant he was breathing on his own. He was alive. She ran to him and held his head.

"You don't get to die, you hear me?" She whispered, kissing his forehead, "You don't get to do this Parker, you weren't supposed to be the first twin to go."

Ellie couldn't help but remember the fights they used to have about her having to die before him because she had been the first to go out of their mother's womb. She always said it would be him first, and he always argued it should be her because she was older.

"Ellie," he got to say before he started coding again. He was in the ambulance before she could even realize it, and she was just sitting on the floor.

"Ellie, we have to go." She looked up to see Allison with her arm spread out, waiting for her to take her hand. "They're taking him to Mayflower. Mom and Dad must be there already."

Charlie walked closely to them and gave Allison a weak smile.

"I'll take you guys to the hospital. My car is right there."

Allison and Ellie cuddled up in the back of Charlotte's car. Their sobbing was being melted into the light tunes that played on the radio. Charlie didn't know what to do to help, she knew how they were feeling. It hit a bit too close to home for her liking, but that girl in the back seat hugging her sister, who she had just met a few hours before, was going to be in her life a long time, and the way she decided to treat her and behave on that day were going to be important factors in their partnership later on.

They arrived at the hospital just seconds after the ambulance, a distraught Jackson helped the paramedics pull his brother out of the bus, and he and Mindy started working on him as soon as they were inside. Hospital policy normally prevented family members from working on family members, but it was the middle of the night, and he was the only trauma surgeon on call. The waiting room quickly started filling up with police officers. Claudia and

Richard Benzinni were received with a wave of silence as they walked into the room looking for their daughters.

"Dad," Ellie fell into her father's arms, crying as soon as they reached them. Richard held onto her tightly but didn't keep his eyes off his youngest daughter, who sat on the floor like a child looking out of a glass window.

"Elizabeth, compose yourself and tell me what happened," The feeling of wanting to get justice roamed through Claudia's veins. It roamed a little too much at that moment when what was needed was their mother there, not the police commissioner.

"He was shot twice in the chest, Ali got there fairly quickly, she did CPR, but he coded twice, they got him back, and Jackson and Mindy are operating now. It doesn't look good, Mom."

"Were there any witnesses?"

"I don't know, Mom, I… when I got there, I was the last to arrive," she tried to recompose herself in her dad's arms, but the way her mother was looking at her only made it worse. "I didn't have time to ask. I was too occupied trying to keep my dying brother awake." And with that, she stormed off to the bathroom.

"Claudia… you ha.." But before Richard could finish, Claudia cut him off.

"I'm going to ask around to see who knows something," and before Richard could get another word out of his mouth, she was gone. He quickly set his path back to Allison who he saw was talking to a young blond woman.

"Allison," he called out her name, and she looked up at him with sad, dark eyes. She quickly got up and hugged her father like she never had before.

"Eve, has anyone called Eve?" She cried, thinking about her poor nieces.

"Two officers were sent to her house about ten minutes ago. She should be on her way here at any moment."

"What about the girls?"

"I...I don't know."

"Oh my god, Dad, please tell me she isn't bringing the girls here," but before Richard could say anything, a tear-stained Eve walked in through the front door, Maia and Hailey asleep one on each side of her arms and Alex still wearing her pajamas and holding a teddy bear by her side.

As soon as Alex saw her aunt and grandpa, she rushed to hug them, not having any idea of what was going on. Allison picked her up in her arms as soon as she reached them, and Richard went to take the twins from Eve. As soon as she did, Eve ran into Ellie's arms, and they cried as they hugged each other tightly.

"Aunt Ali, is something bad going on?" Alex wasn't that small. She was old enough to understand that a hospital full of police officers in the middle of the night wasn't a good thing.

"Not yet, Alex, but if something bad happens, we'll talk about it. For now, why don't I introduce you to my new partner." Allison took Alex to meet Charlie as Richard sat down in a chair, making sure the twins didn't wake up.

It didn't take long for Jackson to come out. The fact that it didn't take long was a really bad thing. Charlie, who was playing with Alex and her teddy bear, looked over at Allison, who also looked at her. They both knew what that meant.

"Alex, stay here with Charlie while I go get some snacks, please." Allison tried not to break down as she went over to her dad and picked the twins up, laying them down on the bench beside Charlie. As she was about to open her mouth, Charlie spoke.

"I'm not going anywhere. I'll be right here with the three of them until you need me to." Allison tried to smile as wide as she could and went to where all her family was breaking down to tears. She could see over the glass window how Eve screamed in pain while Ellie tried to hold her. Mom cried, facing away from everyone, and Dad was trying to recompose himself before going in. Jackson was in the other room throwing things, crying while Mindy tried to calm him down but being careful not to get too close. Allison didn't know what to do, who to go to help, who to comfort.

She looked back at Charlie, who was playing with Alex. She was begging her to turn around and somehow tell her what she had to do. She stared waiting, and when she was about to turn around and give up, Charlie looked up, and their eyes locked. Charlie gave her a small smile, and for Allison, it seemed like the answer to all her questions. She turned around and went into the room where Jackson was breaking down.

Jackson was fifteen when Allison was born, he took care of her as any big brother would, but there were times where he went far and beyond for her, for her, and for Ellie and Parker. And even though they were fifteen years apart, Allison knew Jackson enough to know he was blaming himself for not having been able to save his little brother, as Allison was too blaming herself for not having been able to do more to stop his bleeding or get there sooner. They both blamed themselves, which is why when Allison went into the room, they both broke into tears hugging each other.

That week before the funeral was miserable. Allison wasn't allowed to take days off, so Charlotte tried to make her week the easiest possible. She made sure they weren't called into any disturbing calls unless extremely necessary, and she made sure Allison would laugh at least once a day, which was hard.

Eve was destroyed, and Ellie and her daughter Olivia had been staying at their house to take care of the girls while Eve took the time to mourn. Alex kind of understood what had happened, but the twins were too young, and someone had to entertain them and make sure they were okay. Claudia was taking Parker's death really hard, she hadn't left her room for three days, and rumors had started to go around that she was going to retire, though none of her kids had taken the courage to ask about it.

The funeral hurt much more than they would have thought. It was a military funeral. Too emotional for Eve, she was done crying, or that is what she was trying to convince herself in order to not break down in front of little Alex, who had insisted on going to her dad's funeral.

Allison sat beside Olivia, who was leaning her head on her aunt's shoulder, looking for some support. Ali held her little hand tightly and looked back, searching for Charlie, and just as she had promised, she was sitting amongst many other officers all in their official uniforms. Ellie had her eyes closed, trying not to think about what was going on, and Jackson just caressed her back, trying to help however he could.

On that day, Allison decided she hated the color black. She didn't want to see her nieces and nephews wear black ever again. They cried again, nearly as hard as they had cried the day he died, nearly.

As Eve, Ellie, Claudia, and Richard thanked the people who gave their condolences, Allison held her nieces' hands and headed outside. Olivia tried not to cry, holding her right hand, and Alex cleaned away her tears, holding the left one. As they walked down the steps, Alex let go of her hand and ran to Charlie, who hugged her tightly. Even though she was only seven years old, Alex would never forget how great Charlie was with her that night.

Allison smiled, walking towards her, but before she could get to them, Olivia started pulling her hand to not get closer. Ali couldn't help but think how weird that was. Her ten-year-old niece wasn't one to pull away from meeting new people, but when she turned around to look at her, she could see in her eyes she wanted to cry.

She knelt down, embracing her, and Olivia gave her little body out and cried her eyes out. Alex and Charlie came to them, and while Alex comforted her older cousin, Ali looked up at Charlie.

"Can you please go and get my sister?" She whispered, and Charlie quickly nodded and headed inside.

"I didn't want to cry in front of Aunt Eve. I'm so sorry," she said into Allison's ear, and that made her aunt hug her even stronger while still holding Alex's hand.

Ellie quickly ran outside and picked Olivia up in her arms.

"I'll see you at home," And they quickly left. It didn't take Eve long to come out, and both Alex and her left to get the twins.

Even though it was a hard day, they had opted to have lunch together at home like always. Jackson, Mindy, their two boys with Allison were the first to arrive, and when they all did and sat down, they all broke down again, seeing that empty seat that would never be filled with Parker again.

3 KEEP MOVING FORWARD

"Olivia, please watch the twins one second," Eve asked her while she quickly put Alex's hair into ponytails.

Ellie and Olivia had now been staying with Eve and the girls for three weeks. After the funeral, Eve decided it was time to keep Parker in her heart forever but pull forward for her girls, and Ellie was being a great help. Managing four-year-old twins was a real race for money, and even though Eve was trying to adjust as quickly as possible to being a single parent Ellie's and even Olivia's help was being incredible.

Allison tried to help as much as she could. She would buy groceries and take the girls out on walks when she was off work, although that week, she hadn't been around the house at all because she and Charlie were on an undercover operation.

"I'm so done with this operation," Allison complained for the sixth time, throwing herself on the dirty sofa she had been sleeping on all week.

"Hey, if you're done, I'll just look for another rookie. I assure you any of them will be running at the chance of an undercover op so soon in their careers," Charlie kept on writing her notes from last night down in the notepad.

"Sorry, I'm just tired and want to see my family."

"Ali, I know, but this has to be over soon. There have been 15 reported rapes in 5 days, all in this same club, it couldn't have just stopped suddenly."

"What if they were just tourists passing by and aren't here anymore?"

"Detective Jameson said if we didn't find anything by Saturday night, it would be over, it's two more nights, and at least I'm having fun. I thought you were too."

And, of course, she was. Charlie and her only had to spend all night in the club dancing around and having fun together. They were having a blast even though every single word spoken was heard by three officers in a truck parked behind the back entrance.

"You know I'm also having fun. I mean, if we could have actual alcohol, it would be even better, but I understand why our judgment shouldn't be tampered with."

"Glad you understand," Charlie mocked her, throwing the notepad at her. "Check to see if I'm missing something."

Allison pretended to read something and looked over at Charlie, who was getting ready to have a shower.

"Excuse me miss training officer, you're missing something really important."

"What? Are you serious? I read over them twice" She ran in her towel, grabbing the notepad back and reading quickly through her notes.

"You forgot to write about the amazing woman you danced with all night."

"You idiot," she threw the notepad back at Allison, and after pulling her tongue out at her like a three-year-old, she ran back to the bathroom.

Soon enough, Ali heard the water running and decided to give Jackson a call to see how he was doing, but to her surprise, it wasn't him who picked up the phone.

"Good morning, brother," she sang into the phone.

"It's me, Aunt Allison." She quickly recognized her youngest nephew's voice but was puzzled because she was nearly 100% sure that middle school had started about three hours earlier.

"Why aren't you in school?" She questioned him.

"We had a trip to the NYPD headquarters, but Dad didn't want me to go, so I'm just at home doing some homework."

"Emm… How come?" Allison could kind of figure out her brother's reasoning for not letting Peter go on the trip but thought the measure was a bit too much.

"After Uncle Parker died, dad told Jamie he never wanted to hear any of us talk about being a New York City police officer ever again." her nephew sounded kind of bummed, and she understood.

Peter was way too young to think about what he'd actually be in the future outside of the fantasies his imagination could let him be but not having the chance of being part of something so big in their family was a great worry for Allison when she didn't know whether to choose policing as a line of work or not.

"And how do you feel about that?"

"I don't really mind. I've always wanted to be a doctor like Mom and Dad, but I know Jamie had been seriously looking to go into the marines to then get into the NYPD, but I guess he'll have to look for another line of work."

Allison heard Charlie turn the water off, so she was quick to end the conversation.

"Okay, buddy, well tell dad I called and also tell Jamie I'll call him as soon as I can and talk to him about this."

She hung up and went to the shower to get ready herself. When she was done, they both went out for lunch.

"Who were you talking to when I was in the shower?" Charlie wondered, taking the first bite out of her food.

"My nephew was banned by my brother to go to the NYPD headquarters on a school trip."

"You have got to be kidding," Charlotte was so perplexed that a string of cheese from the pizza she was eating hung from her mouth.

"Clean your mouth," she laughed, handing her a napkin. "And no, from what Peter has told me, he doesn't want the boys to follow in the family's footsteps."

"But aren't your nephews like babies?"

"The youngest is twelve, and Jamie is turning fifteen soon. Apparently, he was looking forward to continuing the family business."

"He's really young. In two years, he'll probably want to be something else."

"You were like 17 when you did your police exams. Did you want to be a stripper?" She laughed.

Charlie had always wanted to be a police officer, ever since she could remember, even though she knew that decision would cost her her family.

"No, always wanted to be a cop," she was sincere, "I think I watched too many police shows growing up."

They spent their lunch talking about everything and anything. Allison often thought about the fact that the woman sitting in front of her knew more about her than any other person in the world apart from her family. They had connected, and Ali was grateful to whoever was above that one of Parker's last things he had done before dying was putting Charlotte in her life. He had given her a guardian angel.

On the other side of town, Claudia and Richard were having a heated argument.

"I'm not retiring, Richard, not for many years, so get that thought out of your head," Claudia shouted, sitting back in her chair.

"Our son has died for god's sake, he died because of us, we have three grand-daughters without a dad because we decided to bring the work home, they followed after us" Richard was heartbroken since the death of Parker, he felt responsible. He was the first to join the force.

"He died doing the job he loved, Parker loved being a police officer, and I'm sure if he could live his life again, he would choose his same life."

"I'm sure he would have chosen another line of work if he knew he could see his daughters grow up and walk them down the aisle."

"He would have never met Eve if he hadn't been working as an officer."

"This is OUR fault, Claudia, don't try to see your way around this. Our son wouldn't be dead if we had chosen to be teachers."

"Grandpa, my dad was a teacher, and he also died." Claudia and Richard stopped the screaming when they saw Olivia standing in the doorway.

"Sorry, honey, you didn't have to hear that" Richard picked his granddaughter up and hugged her tightly.

"Uncle Parker loved his job. He always told us how much fun he had and that he wouldn't change it for anything in the world" Richard kissed her forehead and put her down on the floor. "I'm sure he's sad that he won't be with us anymore, but Uncle Parker did a lot of good things when he was here, and he put a lot of bad guys away."

"Yes, he did," Claudia knelt down to be at Olivia's height. "He did a lot of good for this town like your Mom also does, and Aunt Allison will do."

"And Uncle Jackson and Auntie Mindy, I mean they save people's lives, you all do," Olivia hugged her grandma and ran back out to the backyard where her cousins played football.

All the kids spent a lot of time with their grandpa. Richard had had to have a babysitter take care of his children nearly all their lives, so he was grateful to be able to look after his grandchildren while their parents were at work.

"I'm sorry, Claudia" Richard kissed his wife gently and stepped back. "I'm sorry I brought it up," And with that, he left to play with the kids outside.

Claudia watched from inside how her husband threw himself on the floor, letting the twins climb on him. She had a heart even though her children believed she didn't. It broke her heart knowing that those girls were never going to be able to play like that with their dad, but she knew that her son died doing the job he had wanted to do since he was old enough to think.

Allison and Charlie had just left the station after giving their briefing of the night before. The agent in charge of the operation had suggested for them to try and dance more separated. According to him, it seemed like they were a couple which was probably the reason why no boys approached them.

That night Ali and Charlie barely spoke. They watched each other from opposite sides of the bar, and when they thought the night was going to go unhinged, a muscular guy sat next to Charlie.

"Hey beautiful, you're awfully alone tonight," Charlie had to try hard not to gag when the guy put his hand on her arm.

"Yeah, wasn't really feeling it tonight."

"I've been watching you for a few nights. I see that girl you're usually dancing with sitting right across from us looking at us. Did you guys have a girl fight?" Allison heard what he was saying through the intercom, so she quickly grabbed her drink and went to talk to a girl who was alone.

"That is or was my girlfriend, I'm not sure," Charlie tried to improvise as best as she could. "I don't want to be exclusive, and she's too jealous to let me have fun for one night, so I just told her to leave me alone, but she doesn't seem to want to."

"Why don't you and I get out of here and leave that bitch alone?" his hand was getting lower by the second, and Allison, who was watching from afar, was getting nervous, but Charlie seemed to have the hang of it.

"As much as I'd love to, I'm crazy about that girl, so thank you very much for the offer, but I have to say no." Charlie was following the plan, she was doing as they were told, she now had to say she was going to the bathroom.

"I promise you won't regret it," He put his hand on her thigh, and she politely declined.

"I'm sure I wouldn't, but I'm going to go to pee, and then I'm going to go home alone and think about my relationship but thank you." She smiled at him and went down the stairs towards the bathroom.

Allison saw how he looked at her, making sure she wouldn't follow, and started to go down the stairs again.

"Suspect is moving down the stairs," she whispered, so the police officers heard her through the intercom. "I'm following, Charlotte. Be careful."

"You too, Allison."

She went down slowly, making sure he didn't see her, but he didn't go into the girls' toilet he went into the boys. Allison was confused. She really thought it was him. As she was about to communicate that it wasn't him, she was grabbed and pulled into a bathroom stall.

"GET OFF ME!" she shouted. She kicked and screamed until he put one hand over her mouth and tried to pull her pants down, but Ali wasn't scared, she knew she had back up.

"You little bitches like to fight so hard, but you can't do anything against a man like me" And with that, the door flung open and Charlie pushed him to the floor.

"Ali, you okay?" She asked, holding him onto the floor and cuffing him.

"Yeah, I knew you were coming," They smiled at each other as Allison pulled her pants up and the rest of the officers flooded the club.

4 WORK

Allison and Charlie couldn't help but spend every off-work second together. They had been to the movies, to a concert, to multiple restaurants around and outside of the city, they had even gone to a Bachelorette party by accident one night. They were together all the time and only separated when they decided it was time to go home to sleep.

"So, I'll be seeing you tomorrow," They had partied a bit too hard that night, celebrating that an older officer was retiring, all the precinct was there, and Allison and Charlie had been the last to leave the party. They were now saying good night at Allison's apartment.

"You'll be seeing me in about six hours, so make sure you sleep it off, I want you 100% for tomorrow" Charlie helped her open the door.

"I'll always be 100% for you." Ali hugged her tightly and then walked into the apartment building. Charlie couldn't help but smile like an idiot at her. If you looked closely, you could see the first symptoms of love working their way up her body into her eyes.

Charlie shook her head, trying to rid herself of the thoughts that had made their way into it.

"Focus Reigns, focus," She whispered to herself, making her way to her apartment that was a few minutes away from Ali's.

Just how she had promised Allison was 100%, it was 8am, and any normal human would be dead like Charlotte was, but Allison was happy looking forward to another day at work.

"Good morning, beautiful human" Ali kissed Charlie's cheek before sitting down on the bench.

"How are you so…."

"Pretty? Wonderful? Happy?" Ali tried guessing cutting her off, and Charlie couldn't help but smile.

"I was going to say alive… How are you so alive?"

"You asked me to be 100%, and that is what I shall be."

Charlie grunted before buttoning up her shirt and walking out of the lockers into roll call.

The morning went by kind of quickly. When they were about to take a break, a call came in through the radio.

"23 David be advised we're receiving a 52, a dispute on West 23rd Street, the suspect could be armed, approach with caution."

"That's us," Charlotte faked smiled, changing lanes. "I was really looking forward to that pizza."

"We're still getting the pizza, Charlie, just a little later."

The dispute was between a man and his boss. The boss was armed, so when he lounged towards Allison, he was quickly arrested. He complained the whole way to the precinct and all way through booking.

"Now we can go and get that pizza," Allison pulled her hair into a ponytail and started making her way outside.

"Hey, meet me in the car. I have to go pee."

The rest of their shift went by fairly quickly. They finished and like always they went out together to get a drink, which turned into dinner and then they spent two hours talking about life in Central Park while people walked around them. The moment Charlie realized she had been staring at Allison's lips for a good five minutes, she quickly stood up and smiled.

"We really should get going if you want to go see your nieces before they go to bed," Allison realized the quick change in attitude that Charlie had had but didn't associate it with the real reason behind what had happened.

"It's okay, Char, I can see them tomorrow. I'm having a good time, I don't want to leave yet."

"I also need to go. I have to have a shower and finish watching this movie I started last night."

"You were with me last night," and when Allison said that, something in her head rang a bell. She thought for a moment that maybe they were spending too much time together, and Charlie wanted to do something else apart from being with her all the time.

"I meant the night before." Charlotte awkwardly smiled.

"You were with me that night too, that night and every other night for like the past two weeks."

"Then it must have been after I got back to the apartment. I mean, I did fall asleep halfway, so it had to be quite late," she tried to fix it, thinking that Ali was catching on to what was happening in her head.

"You don't have to lie, Char, it's okay for you to want to spend some time alone or with someone else. I think since Parker, you've wanted to make sure I was okay and didn't want to leave me, but I'm okay. You really don't have to worry."

"Allison, no, I mean, I love spending time with you, I'm not doing anything I don't want to, I look forward to the shift ending all day because I know it means we get to be together even more," She stopped dead in her tracks when she said that. She couldn't help but think that it had sounded like a love declaration.

"You're blushing," Allison teased, trying to break the silence that had made its way between them.

"You idiot, what I mean to say is I like spending time with you. I just think it'd be okay if you went to see your nieces today."

"It's a great idea," Ali didn't feel that pressuring her was a good idea, so she decided to do what she was told and went to see her nieces and Eve.

They ended their day there, Allison took the subway to Eve's house, and Charlie walked to her apartment, hoping that her head would clear up.

Ellie

Early in the morning, Ellie and her partner Tom Johns were called into the 23rd precinct. The fact that the call had been made to her was a courtesy because her sister was involved made her nervous. She hadn't seen herself in this situation ever before.

"Detective Benzinni, Detective Johns, thank you for coming" The sergeant that had replaced Parker smiled at them. "I'm Sergeant Maria Wells, I didn't really know what to do, but if I tell the Captain, he'll have to report to Commissioner Benzinni, and I'm just…Allison is a colleague, and I've known Reigns for a while now, and they're both great. I just didn't want to make things worse."

"It's perfect, Sergeant, thank you." Ellie smiled genuinely back at her…What had her sister and her partner done?

"Let's go in here to talk." Tom and Ellie both followed Sergeant Wells into the room and sat down in front of her.

"So what happened?" It was early in the morning, and Ellie and Tom were both anxious to go home after finishing their shift.

"Yesterday before ending their shift Officer Reigns and Officer Benzinni were called to a dispute, one of the offenders got apprehended after having threatened Officer Benzinni with a knife, they booked him, and everything was okay until a few hours ago when he was getting released and when collecting his belongings he claimed that something was missing."

"A watch? A wallet? What was missing?"

"He claims he had five grand in his wallet prepared to pay his workers that day when he got the wallet back, the five grand were missing," Sergeant Wells was new to being in charge. She had just been promoted and didn't want to screw anything up, especially with the commissioner's daughter.

"Is there any chance he was lying?" Ellie knew Allison couldn't have taken that money and didn't think Charlotte could have taken it from how she was the numerous times they had seen each other, but she didn't know her to an enough profound level to vouch for her as she could for her sister.

"We know he took out five grand at the ATM a few minutes before his arrest, he could have given the money to someone or misplaced it, but the official protocol is to start an investigation."

"I can vouch for my sister Sergeant Wells. I don't know Officer Reigns enough to tell you it wasn't her, but I think we should forget this meeting ever happened, and you should tell your Captain as soon as possible," Ellie didn't know what to do, but she did know Allison hadn't taken that money, so the best thing that came to mind was to let an official investigation clear their names.

"I'm sorry about this. I just didn't want to push them under the bus unless necessary."

"It's okay, Sergeant Wells, but next time don't give special treatment to any officer because of where he or she comes from, though I do appreciate the heads up, it wasn't the correct thing to do."

They left quickly after that, and each headed home. Ellie quietly got into her parents' house, looking at the watch on her wrist, it was 4:30am. She went into the room where she knew her daughter was sleeping and kissed her forehead softly, making sure she wouldn't wake up, and left a note on her bedside like she always did when she worked night shifts.

Before she could leave the house to go to her home, which was right next door, her mother turned the light on, scaring her half to death.

"Mom, jeez, you scared me," She whispered, trying not to make noise.

"Sorry, didn't mean to startle you. I heard you come in. You finished later than usual today, had a big case?"

"No, actually" She didn't know if it was better for her to hear from her or from the Captain the next day. "You're going to hear about it tomorrow morning, so I guess I'll just tell you."

"What did you do?"

"For once, I didn't do anything, it's Allison."

"I knew the female partnership would be a problem."

"It's not that…Well, kind of not. Some money disappeared from booking, it was Allison's case."

"How much?"

"Five grand"

"Your sister didn't take that money."

"I know, Mom, they'll put her and her partner on suspension until the investigation has concluded, and when they've been cleared, they'll be back."

And that was exactly what happened

5 TROUBLE

That morning Allison and Charlie arrived at work together like every day, but the morning started out very differently when they were asked by the captain to join him at his office.

They looked at each other really confused, they hadn't done anything wrong, their last shift had been rather boring.

"Sit down, officers," Captain Martinez said as he shut the door. When they turned around, they realized there were another three people in the room. Their Sergeant, who they were good friends with, and two men they hadn't met before.

They sat in the two available chairs. Allison couldn't help but be nervous, she hadn't even been on the job for more than a month, and she was already in trouble. Charlie, on the other hand, was more optimistic. She thought that maybe they wanted them on a special operation or something, she definitely didn't expect what was about to happen.

"Officer Reigns, Officer Benzinni, this is Dawson James and Frederic George from internal affairs," Charlotte's face changed drastically. Ali didn't catch on that quickly.

"I don't understand," Charlotte sounded as confused as could be expected from an innocent person. "What happened?"

"Last night, you arrested a Harry Long on West 23rd Street after a dispute with a co-worker, is that right?" The older man from the pair of IA agents asked. Allison was still confused.

"Yes, but sorry, I'm just really confused. What is going on?" Allison looked at Charlie, looking for an explanation, but as an officer with a few years of experience, she knew that what was best in those situations was for them to keep their mouth shut and just answer the questions asked by the agents truthfully.

"Benzinni, Internal affairs is here to investigate something that happened last night with your arrest," Sergeant Wells tried explaining to the rookie. "Just answer their questions, and everything will be fine."

Allison nodded, still not understanding what could have gone wrong with that arrest, it was simple and straightforward, or that was what she thought.

"Can either of you walk me through the arrest and his booking?"

"We were about to go for our lunch break when we got called into a dispute on 23rd Street. When we got there, we saw that Mr. Long was armed with a knife, so we drew our guns, kept our distance, and tried talking him into leaving the knife on the floor."

"Do you know what the dispute was about?" The youngest IA agent now talked, taking notes on his notepad.

"It was a work dispute, the other man was Mr. Long's employee. When we questioned him, he just said there had been a disagreement but didn't want to press charges" This time, Allison was the one to answer.

"Why was he arrested then?"

"While trying to talk him out of the knife, he went towards Officer Benzinni, so I took out my taser and tased him." Charlie took back the explaining, giving Allison a look she understood to mean *to let her talk*. "He was handcuffed, and after questioning the employee, he was brought into booking."

"Were both of you together at all times while being in the precinct?"

They took a moment to think. Allison quickly remembered that Charlotte had gone to the bathroom before heading back out, but that was the only time they had separated. Charlotte wasn't so quick to remember, though, so Allison thought she would help and just tell the truth.

"At all times except for a moment when Officer Reigns went to the bathroom while I started up the car," She said truthfully but got scared when at that moment both agents stood up, closing their notepads, they turned to look at the captain, and he also stood up.

"In that case, Officer Reigns, Officer Benzinni, you are temporarily suspended pending the investigation of Mr. Long's case," Captain Martinez explained, proceeding to ask for their badges and guns.

"What? But what the hell happened? We haven't even been told what happened" Charlie was nervous.

"You will each be questioned separately now. You will know what happened" Maria tried helping them out. "Just don't make it difficult, Officer Reigns, give in your badge and gun, and you will be getting them back as soon as this has been cleared up." It was in that moment Allison realized Sergeant Wells and Charlie had more than a working relationship. She looked at both of them confused, as she took off her badge and handed it with her gun to the captain. Charlotte did the same before storming out of the office.

"So I guess you'll be first, Officer Benzinni." All Allison wanted to do was hug Charlie and ask her what to do. She was confused and didn't really understand anything, but she knew that wasn't an option, so she breathed in deeply a few times and sat on the opposite side of the table where they were setting up a camera.

"You are allowed to ask for a lawyer if you like," The younger one of the two agents smiled, something that Allison had realized hadn't happened before. Suddenly, she remembered something her brother had once told her before graduating from the academy that stuck.

"When in questioning if you have two suspects, always try to find the weak

link first. That will be the one you want to choose to play good cop, bad cop with. The weak link will break first."

"I'm okay. I don't need a lawyer, thank you."

"Okay, so before proceeding, let me tell you what happened."

Allison was finally relieved for a few seconds knowing that she was going to know what had happened.

"Last night someone paid Mr. Long's bail, when being released and getting his things back he claimed five grand had been stolen from his wallet."

"Okay and?" She still didn't understand what all the mess was for.

"He claims he had those five grand when being arrested."

"Wait? Are you suggesting we took the money?"

"We are not suggesting anything officer, we are just here to get all the facts so we can start our investigation."

"Well, I can tell you right now that neither I nor my partner took that money."

"You've known Officer Reigns for a while now, right?"

"A bit over a month"

"Has she expressed in any moment a need for more money or being underpaid or having difficulties at home or someone in her family having any problems?"

"What? No. Charlie, I mean Officer Reigns, didn't take that money, she doesn't need the money, she's fine, she would never do that."

"From our understanding from Sergeant Wells, Officer Reigns and you have a really good relationship, right?"

"Yes, I mean we're colleagues. We are stuck in the same car together for hours on end."

"But you are also good friends outside of work, isn't that right?"

"Yes, I guess. What does that have to do with anything?" Allison was starting to feel pressured to turn on Charlie, and she didn't like the feeling.

"What level of friendship would you say you two have?" Every question made her more confused. What the hell did that have to do with anything?

"I'm not answering that question."

"Would you… Say if Officer Reigns acted in a wrong way in a case, you would report her?"

"Yes, of course."

"Even if that would compromise your relationship?"

"Yes, if my partner did anything that didn't follow the rules, I would report her like I would any other cop."

The 'good cop' agent sat down, and the one who Allison supposed would play 'bad cop' stood up and walked over to her side of the table sitting next to her in the spare chair.

"When we read the case last night, we read some reports on some of your other assignments together, a few weeks ago, both Officer Reigns and yourself worked on an undercover operation, the report, which was written by the detective who worked with you on that case stated that you both worked incredibly well together and had great communication, but he did point out that some nights

Officer Reigns and you acted and looked more like a couple than like partners."

"It was undercover work. I still don't know how this has anything to do with anything."

"Are you and Officer Reigns romantically involved?"

"I think this is way out of line, and I'm going to stop answering questions now." Allison felt like crying, and she didn't know why. She didn't understand why those questions were being asked, she didn't understand her difficulty to say a simple no to that question. They weren't romantically involved, of course, they weren't. They were colleagues, friends. Nothing more.

"In that case, Officer Benzinni, you are free to go home. From this moment on, you are temporarily suspended pending investigation. If you are found not guilty, your badge and gun will be returned to you, and you will return to full active duty. Do you understand?"

"Yes," And with that, she stood up and left the room.

When she closed the door behind her, she saw Charlie sitting on a chair waiting to be called. She was moving her right leg up and down and was nervously brushing her blonde hair back. Before she could go and talk to her, Ellie appeared out of nowhere, grabbing her arm.

"You can't talk to her right now."

"What are you doing here?" Now she was even more confused. Why was Ellie there?

"Let's talk on the way home," And that is what they did, they got in the car and drove in silence for a while, but Allison couldn't hold it in any longer.

"Did you know about this?" She asked angrily, having a feeling that she knew all about it.

"Your sergeant called me in last night. She didn't know what to do because you're the commissioner's daughter, and she didn't want to act wrongly."

"So you knew and didn't give me a heads up?" Now she was really angry. "Do you know how fucked up that interrogation was? I was so fucking confused."

"If I had told you anything, you would have told Charlotte."

"And?"

"How do you know it wasn't her who took the money? We all have problems in our personal lives that people at work don't know about."

"You're kidding, right?" Ali felt offended and didn't exactly know why but her sister doubting Charlie hurt her more than she could explain. "Charlie didn't take that money."

"I know you feel like you know her really well, Ali, but it hasn't been much more than a month since you've met her. She could have things in her personal life you don't know about."

"It wasn't her," she said clearly and with a bit of anger in her voice. "I'm 100% sure."

"I'm not saying it was, but if it wasn't you and it wasn't her… Who took the money?"

"Have they even checked the cameras?" Ellie gave her a secretive look, and glanced around. Allison realized that she was asking her to discuss something she couldn't but insisted by not taking her eyes off her sister who breathed in and told her.

"They were disconnected for five minutes. The image went off when Charlotte went back into the precinct and connects exactly when she is going back out" Allison didn't doubt in any moment, she knew it wasn't Charlie. It couldn't be.

"Okay, so that is oddly timed, but Ellie, I assure you it isn't her."

Her sister just smiled sweetly at her. Ellie knew Ali had forged a good friendship with her partner, they spent much more time than normal together, and they seemed to work great together, but she was also scared that her sister could have gotten herself into a situation she didn't really control, maybe inside she knew her partner had stolen that money, but her heart didn't let her brain believe it. She crossed her fingers, hoping that Charlotte would be cleared because if it had been her, Allison would be distraught.

Ellie dropped Allison at her apartment like she had asked. After saying goodbye and walking up the stairs to keep in shape, she locked her door and threw herself onto the sofa. She closed her eyes, waiting for her phone to light up with a message from Charlotte, but she fell asleep waiting.

Banging on her door woke her up. She looked through the hole and was relieved when she saw Charlie on the other side. When she opened, an angry Charlie walked in, stomping her feet.

"What the hell was that interview about? Why didn't you answer the phone? I've called you like twelve times. You know it wasn't me, right?" She kept talking and pacing from one side of the living room to the other. "Allison, you know it wasn't me, right?"

Charlie looked defeated, and for the first time since she had met her, Allison saw that little 22-year-old girl who was just a child growing up surrounded by a huge mess of a world.

"Allison," her face turned serious all of a sudden, "Why are you looking at me like that? It wasn't me." she started crying, and Ali ran to pull her into a hug.

"Of course, I know it wasn't you," she softly took her face into her hands and smiled. "I haven't had any doubt at any moment, Charlie."

"They made me feel like I had done it in that interview," her breathing was fast, and anyone could see how fast her mind was going. "I'm not even supposed to be here. Why am I here?"

"Char, breath, it's okay. It's going to be okay, I promise" Allison caressed her cheek lightly with her thumb, but instead of calming her down, she pulled back.

"They said that Detective Jameson said we looked like a couple instead of partners," Allison bit her lip, knowing that Charlie wasn't going to take that comment nicely.

"I know. They told me he wrote it on his report."

"And they asked if we were involved romantically," she looked down at the floor, trying to organize the thousands of thoughts that were running around in her mind.

"What the hell does that have to do with anything?"

"They asked me the same questions, Charlie, but it's all going to be fine, they'll figure out what happened, and we'll be back at work in no time. Let's take these days as vacation days. I'll make us some breakfast."

"No, no, I have to go," Charlie gave a forced smile. "I shouldn't have come, and I'm sorry for being a crap training officer today, you…If this was confusing for me, it must have been really confusing for you. I'm really sorry."

"We were both rookies in this situation, Char, we handled it fine, and I promise it's going to be okay."

They ended up doing the right thing, Charlie went to her house, and they each had breakfast alone, staring at the tv. They were both confused, slightly scared, and both trying to figure out what to could have happened.

The investigation took longer than expected. It was Friday, and Allison was on her way to have dinner at her childhood home with her family. She missed Charlie, it seemed stupid, but they had made sure to keep the rule of no contact between them after their encounter the other day.

Allison wasn't really paying attention to what was happening around her at the table. The kids were running around while the adults prepared everything.

"Hey, kiddo," Her dad kissed her head and sat beside her holding her hand. "You seem a little absent."

"I'm just nervous because our investigation hasn't concluded yet. I really thought it wouldn't take much longer than a day to figure out what happened"

"Sometimes, these things are slow. If they are out of leads, they will ask other agents to pitch in. IA takes the time they need."

"I know, but I just hate not being able to communicate with my partner, not being able to go to work."

"Well, your nieces are loving having you at home."

Allison laughed, looking at the two little ones running after their older cousins.

She had been going over every morning, taking them out to the park and to the pier. She was enjoying her "vacation days," but she wanted everything to be sorted out as quickly as possible and to get back to work. To get back to Charlie.

"I... I know, and I'm grateful to be able to spend some quality time with them, but I want this to be sorted out. I hate not having an explanation to what happened"

They started eating soon after that. Apart from the casual conversation starter, they were rather quiet. Things were a bit tense between Ellie and Allison, and everyone knew and noticed, even the kids.

"Why are Aunt Ellie and Aunt Allison angry at each other?" Alex asked but was quickly told off by her mother, so she closed her mouth and sat back in her chair.

Olivia feeling bad for her cousin being punished, spoke up.

"Aunt Allison is angry because her partner stole money, and my Mom knew but di…."

"Olivia." Ellie was quick to shut her up, but not enough.

"Are you kidding me?" Allison stood up, turning to look at Ellie.

"I didn't say Charlotte stole it. She was just overhearing when I told Eve what was going on."

"She only said that it wasn't you who had stolen that money, Ali," Eve tried to help, but it didn't land.

"It wasn't my partner either," she said, still looking at Ellie. "I really don't know how to tell you, it wasn't Charlotte, I'd put my career on the line to assure that."

"Oh, come on, Allison," and finally, the matriarch talked, she had tried not to comment on what her daughter was going through, but she'd had enough of her innocence. "You met the woman a month ago, you can't know if something is going on in her life and she might need that money. Don't be so naïve."

"I'm not naïve. Officer Reigns is my partner and my friend, and I know for sure it wasn't her who took that money. If she needed money, she would ask me before doing something like that," She defended Charlie to the best of her abilities.

"You just can't be sure, darling." Her dad making that comment made it for her. She got up and left the house without saying goodbye.

She drove to that restaurant they had gone to on her first day, hoping for some peace and a good hamburger, but when she went in, she had to stop herself. There she was. Looking tired, wearing her hair in a small ponytail and eating a hamburger bigger than herself.

She didn't intend to meet Charlie. That couldn't be disobeying the rules, right? She wanted to do the right thing, not just for herself but for Charlie too, but when she saw her wipe a tear away, she didn't think twice. She popped her hoodie up, trying to cover herself up as much as she could, and sat in front of her in the booth.

"Allison, what the hell?" Charlotte tried not to talk too loud but was surprised to see her there. "How did you know where I was?"

"I didn't," she whispered. "I came here to grab lunch and saw you."

"Someone could be watching us, Allison. We shouldn't be talking."

"Go to the bathroom in two minutes," And before Charlie could get another word in, Allison had left into the bathroom.

She looked around, seeing if anything looked suspicious, but no one caught her eye, there were only five other people inside, and there weren't many cars in the parking lot. She breathed in.

Charlie was her training officer, she was the one who was meant to do the right thing, but her need to see her and talk to her was greater than the responsibility she felt to learn from her at that moment.

She went towards the bathroom as cautiously as possible and knocked three times, the door opened slowly, and a hand-pulled her in. As soon as they were in front of each other, they hugged tightly. Ali kissed Charlie's forehead while holding her with a firm grip.

"I missed you way too much," she said sincerely, and Charlotte couldn't help but smile. She, too, had missed her partner.

"I did too, Ali, but we really shouldn't be talking to each other. We could screw this investigation up."

"They're taking too long, right?" Allison asked, not sure if she wanted an answer.

"Yes," she was honest with her. "This should have been sorted out already, and I have a bad feeling that if they don't figure out what happened, they are going to fire me as damage control."

"I won't let that happen."

Charlie couldn't help but smile seeing Allison's small angry face saying that.

"That is terribly sweet, but you don't control that, Ali."

"I'm sure my Mom can stop that from happening if it comes to that, but it can't happen, Charlie. You're like the best young cop there is. They aren't just going to get rid of you."

Charlie just hugged her and Allison knew all she wanted was for her not to worry about what would happen to herself.

"It was great seeing you, Ali, but you have to leave before someone finds out we saw each other here today." Allison hugged her even tighter. She didn't want to let go. She wasn't prepared to go back to zero communication.

"There has to be some sort of way for us to talk without them being able to track it if it comes to that"

"The investigation won't go on for much longer Allison, it'll just be a few more days top, for good or for bad" They hugged one last time, and when they were letting go, they got stuck in each other's eyes. Without taking their eyes off each other, they could tell they were smiling.

"I promise everything will be back to normal very soon" Ali hugged her tightly and opened the door leaving a sad yet happy and confused Charlie looking at herself in the mirror.

She left a few minutes after Allison did. She paid Macarena, the waitress and the first person she had met in that city that really never slept, and then got into her car. When she did, it started pouring with rain, and Charlie felt she was in her own personal music video. Her sad songs Spotify playlist played in the background like it had been playing for the last three days.

Allison wasn't having a good time with the suspension, but Charlie had it ten times worst. She had replayed that afternoon in her head over and over again, but all she remembered was her being so focused on how she looked before going out with Allison that she didn't see anything else.

At that moment, she decided that if she got her job back, she would ask for a partner change. Allison wasn't letting her focus on her job. But how could she explain that? Why wasn't she able to focus on her job because of Allison? She had been doing that exact same job since she was eighteen. Why did Allison compromise all of that?

On the other side of town, sitting on her sofa, Allison hid her face under a cushion. She was going to kiss her. She looked at her lips.

What was wrong with her? Allison tried to convince herself that the IA agents had put ideas in her head about Charlie and her being romantic, and that's why it had happened, but she knew she couldn't blame it on that. She had thought about Charlie in a romantic way before, even if she didn't want to admit it.

"DON'T THINK ABOUT HER IN THAT WAY," she screamed into the cushion, trying to let some frustration out.

She started crying. Allison had never felt so confused and frustrated. Charlie was her training officer, even if she had romantic feelings for her, she couldn't act on them, and Charlie didn't even feel the same about her. She groaned, throwing herself back down on the sofa.

Right, when she was going to go into the shower, a knock on the door made her heart rise. Her first thought was Charlie, but when she heard the voice on the other side of the door, she breathed deeply, trying to calm herself down.

"Allison, open up, please." Ellie's voice sounded a bit defeated, and Allison felt bad. "I didn't mean to insinuate that Charlotte had taken that money. Please just let me in."

Allison unlocked the door and let her in without looking at her.

"Forgive me, please. I didn't mean to offend you."

"I shouldn't have been so affected. You are all entitled to an opinion about another officer, especially if you don't know her," she tried derailing the conversation, afraid that her big sister could find out why she was so offended.

"I don't know her, Ali, but you do, and that should be enough," she smiled and hugged her sister. "You're a clever girl, you've always been really bright, and you have good intuition. If you are so sure that it wasn't your partner, that should have been enough for all of us."

"You have to find out what happened Ellie, we need our job back. I need for Char…." She stopped herself before saying too much.

"Allison, she's your t.o" Ellie's voice shared concern, and that was exactly what Allison's older sister was feeling. She was concerned about the intense feelings Allison had shown towards her partner.

Ellie knew how much time they spent together, on and off work, and even though she knew how special it was to find someone with who you could spend every moment with, she was worried about her sister crossing the line on her first months at work for love.

"I know," she looked ashamed, scared, and worried, "I don't… I just need my work back Ellie, I need everything to go back to normal. These days have been messing with my head."

"They should be calling me today letting me know what they're planning to do, for good or for bad tomorrow, you will for sure be back at work. I'm just not sure who you will be going back to work with."

"You can't let it happen, Ellie. You can't let her lose her job."

"I'll try, I promise."

But she didn't have to. Later that day, Ellie received a call, both Allison and Charlie were cleared and could return back to duty the day after. The officer who was at the booking desk had been convicted of stealing the money. He had been doing it for a while, so when he didn't get caught, he got greedy and couldn't stop himself when he saw such a big quantity of money.

6 LIPS

Charlie

Allison and Charlie were back on the job, the first shift back, Charlie got into work a little bit earlier and went to speak to Sergeant Wells about changing partners, but she didn't like the idea.

"María, just pair me up with anyone else, I… I don't work well with Benzinni" Charlie and María had had a short relationship when Charlie first transferred into the precinct. It hadn't ended badly, and they were good friends.

"You know if I change Benzinni because of a personal request, I have to inform the captain, and you'll both be questioned."

"Can't you just change us so she gets to know another officer? I don't know, María, please, do it for me." Charlie didn't like using their old relationship to get anything, but she had to change partners, she wasn't focused when riding with Allison.

"Tell me why."

"Why what?" She knew what she wanted her to confess, but she wasn't going to, she hadn't fallen for any of her partners. She didn't like being that kind of person.

"Why do you want to change partners? Every report I've read just indicates that you guys work great together, you are clean, you follow the rules, and because of your ages and looks, you two make an amazing pairing for undercover work."

"I just feel like I'm not teaching her like I should."

"I can't change you without giving an official report Charlotte," she said with a frown on her face, María wanted to help her friend, she had just been ascended and wanted her officers to trust her and to count on her, but she couldn't do that favor for Charlie because she would have to reorganize everything and change a partnership that probably didn't want to change.

"Well, that's great" Charlotte nervously bit her lip, turning around to look out of the window where she saw Allison laughing with some of their co-workers.

"Charlie, if there's a problem, have a talk with Benzinni, she seems like a great girl, and you two seemed to be working great. I'm sure you can sort it out, and if by the end of the shift you still think there's no solution, I'll put in your request and try to get it sorted without getting too much attention, but the name Benzinni on any report will be looked at with much more precision than any other."

"Yeah, thanks, María." she smiled at her friend and left the room, going into the locker room where she ran into Allison, who was changing.

"Hey," Charlie saw how nervous Allison was to see her. Since they got the news they were to go back to work two days earlier, they hadn't talked even though they could. "How come you were in with María?"

"Just had to talk something out. Get changed quickly, I'll be waiting in the car," And with that, she left as quickly as she had entered, leaving a really confused Allison buttoning up her shirt.

The week went by with barely any conversation between them. They stopped meeting out of work, and when they spoke at work, it was only about the work itself. Charlie was doing her best to not be tented by Allison's confused face, she knew she should have given her an explanation, but she knew if she looked at her, she wouldn't be able to explain it. But Allison wasn't going to be patient much longer.

Charlie was eating a large pizza all by herself when an insistent banging on her door made her slowly go for her gun, but before she could unlock the safe, she turned around.

"Open up right now," Allison's pissed voice made her breathe in deeply. She knew her partner, she knew it wouldn't take her long to look for an explanation to her attitude the last few days, but she didn't expect it to be at her house on their day off.

"Benzinni, it's my off day. You better have a good reason to be here on the day I'm meant to be resting."

"Officer Reigns, open the fucking door" And with that, she did as she was told, and an angry Allison walked in and started pacing back and forth when Charlie closed the door. "Just so we're clear, I'm not here as your rookie, or your partner or nothing that is related to work."

"Okay," Charlie tried to say as calmly as possible, sitting down on the sofa and inviting Allison to do the same.

"I need an explanation Char, I… I haven't been able to sleep properly all week trying to figure out what I could have done wrong, why you suddenly shut me out, why you won't even look at me" When she said that, she slowly put her hand on Charlie's cheek asking her to look up at her. "What did I do, Charlie?"

But Charlotte couldn't answer. All she did was break into tears. Allison quickly hugged her and held her in her arms, waiting for her to calm down. It took a while for her to finally even her breathing.

"Ali, I'm so sorry," She whispered, still in Allison's arms. Ali caressed her hair gently while still holding her tightly, making sure she didn't feel alone.

"It's okay, it's okay."

Allison

Allison left her apartment that day without any kind of explanation from Charlie, but she knew they were back to being okay, and for the moment, that was enough for her.

A few weeks went by, and their usual dynamic was back in place. They'd do their shift, and after work, they'd go out for any random plan. That night they had decided on having a quick beer at a new bar in Brooklyn, and then they would each head home for a good night's sleep.

"What can I get you?" The young waitress smiled eagerly at Charlie, making Allison laugh.

"We'll have two beers, please," Charlie flirted back, trying to annoy her friend, who was still laughing in front of her. "What's wrong with you?" She asked once the waiter had left.

"Does anyone ever not flirt with you?"

"Emm," she pretended to think really hard, which caused even more laughter in Allison, "I think everyone tends to flirt with me."

"Why are you single then?" Allison was genuinely curious. They had a great friendship and had spent hours on end with each other talking about every other stupid thing but had never gotten into the topic of exes.

"I don't think relationships go well with our line of work," Charlie tried not to look at her when she said that. "I tried dating this cop about a year ago, but it just didn't go well."

"María?" Allison was curious to see if what she thought she has seen between them the other day was actually real or not.

"What?"

"Sergeant Wells, that's the cop you dated, right?"

"How? How do you know?" Charlotte was actually confused, they hadn't told anyone they were seeing each other, and they weren't together long enough for anyone to realize, or that was what she thought.

"It was a guess," she laughed it off. "The other day before our IA interviews, I just got a feeling."

"We didn't date for long, but we are good friends."

"Do you mind me asking why you broke up?"

"I had night shifts, and she had mornings, we barely had any time to see each other, and I guess it wasn't really meant to be," Charlie looked up at Allison, who was looking at her with a curious face. "I mean, I guess if I thought it was going to be a long-term thing, I would have tried harder to keep the relationship going."

"I get it," She smiled. "We work a lot of hours, and being on different hour shifts can mess with any couple."

"Yes, it isn't easy," They both locked eyes, "but with the right person it can be." Charlie's eyes slowly made their way to Allison's lips, and a thousand thoughts ran through her mind, a thousand of thoughts that also ran through Allison's mind when she realized she was too looking at her t.o's lips.

Charlie couldn't help but bite her bottom lip, trying to stop herself from doing something she knew she'd regret when they were separated and couldn't work together anymore. But that bite was enough to send Allison's doubts out of the window. She slowly got closer to Charlie, who was suddenly unnerved. Charlie breathed deeply, trying to convince herself that it wasn't a mistake. She felt Allison's breath on her lips and was pushed by a sudden urge to feel her lips. They were going to kiss. After weeks of confusion, they were going to do something that both had wanted deeply but hadn't realized.

"HELP PLEASE HELP!" That scream was followed by what sounded like gunshots. Their lips had briefly touched. For anyone around them, they probably hadn't even touched, but they had felt it, yet the moment they had longed for was suddenly broken by that terrifying sound.

They were both quick to draw their weapons and separate.

"Everyone down," Charlie shouted to everyone in the bar they were in as they both exited.

The first thing they both saw was an LGBTQ+ flag waving on top of the bar where numerous people were lying on the floor. They looked at each other quickly before running over to help the ones who looked worse.

"This is Off Duty Officer Reigns. Badge number 2764. Shots fired at the Metropolitan bar on 559 Lorimer Street. Multiple injuries. Send multiple buses to my location." Charlie quickly called 911 before hanging up and running faster.

Surveying the scene, Allison saw multiple injured people. She watched as Charlie began to aid them. Just as Charlie was about to stop the bleeding from a woman who had been shot in the leg, she saw a man running away from the scene, Her eyes squinted. Allison saw it too, He had a gun

"Benzinni, stop this bleeding. The suspect is fleeing the scene," Allison did as she was told, and Charlie quickly grabbed her phone again. "This is Off Duty Officer Reigns Again. I'm in pursuit of the suspect. He's about 5'11, strong build, blonde hair, wearing a dark green shirt and black trousers."

She ran as fast as she could, pointing her gun and ordering him to stop.

Allison tried to get standbyers to help to put pressure on the wounds as she watched Charlie run after the man. As the ambulances arrived, Allison made sure everyone was attended and ran after Charlie, who was getting to the end of the street. Her heart was racing. She was terrified that the man would turn around and shoot at Charlie, who wasn't wearing a vest.

"Charlie, I'm behind you," she shouted as loudly as she could, and just as Charlie was about to catch him, a car hit her.

Allison stopped dead in her tracks. She couldn't believe what had just happened. It took her a few seconds to realize, but when she did, she ran as fast as she could, tears streaming down her face. Some people had already stopped and were standing next to Charlie, some called 911, and some stood far away, trying to stop their kids from seeing.

"Char, Char?" She screamed when she was getting near her, she saw blood a lot of blood, but she seemed to be awake. She got to her side carefully, trying to assess her injuries. "Charlie, where does it hurt?"

"Al, I'm okay. I hit my head, I think my arm is broken." She was extremely calm, and that only made Allison more nervous.

"The ambulance is coming, you're going to be okay."

"I think I can," She tried to sit up, but Allison was quick to push her back down.

"Don't you dare try to move, you idiot."

Charlie couldn't help but smile even though she was feeling pain all over her body.

"Allison, go and help the people from the bar."

"I'm not moving, Charlotte, just hang on, help will be here in a second." And it was. A few seconds later, one of the ambulances was dispatched, and Charlie was taken to the hospital.

Before leaving, Charlie made Allison stay back to make sure every victim was taken care of, she tried fighting her, but she ended up doing as she was told. She took the last ambulance leaving the scene after a few hours of helping around, and arrived at the hospital relatively quickly.

As Allison looked for her brother or her sister-in-law. On the other side of town, Claudia Benzinni started her press announcement about the incident.

"At 9:02 PM there was an attack in a well known LGBT club in downtown Brooklyn, we don't know the exact number of injuries, but we have a good prognostic that none of the victims were fatal, two off duty officers, Officer Reigns and Officer Benzinni were having dinner at a nearby restaurant and were the first on the scene. Officer Reigns went after the suspect, giving us a good description of the man. While in pursuit, she was hit by a car that didn't see her. She is now in stable condition, and we've locked down all entries to Brooklyn. The suspect had not yet been apprehended, so I will give you a description, so you are vigilant and call 911 if you see anyone matching this description. We are looking for a male suspect about 5'11, strong build, blonde hair, wearing a dark green shirt and black trousers." She breathed in deeply, looking at all those expectant news reporters. "We will not be taking any questions at the moment."

She quickly left the stand and walked into her office, picking up her coat and bag heading to the hospital. In the hospital, Jackson talked to a nervous Allison who insisted on seeing her partner.

"Allison, you will see her when you're allowed to see her. You're not family, I can't let you into observation," Jackson insisted, trying to make his sister see reason.

"But her family isn't here, and they aren't going to come right now, so seriously, just let me go in."

"She hasn't even had all her test done, her arm is splinted, and she's getting checked out neurologically, but she seems okay. Stop hovering and let her rest. Come back in a few hours when she's in her room."

Even though Allison didn't like being told what to do, she listened to her brother. She turned around, annoyed, and decided to go back to her apartment to have a shower and change before heading back.

Charlie

A few hours went by, and Charlie was trying to fall asleep, but the thought of Allison's lips on hers was keeping her awake, they hadn't touched for more than a second, but she could still feel them on hers. Either that or the pavement she basically ate when falling on the ground, she had seen herself in the bathroom mirror a few minutes back, and she looked like hell. She brushed her lips with her fingers trying to go back to the instance before the disaster happened, but someone knocking on the door made her put her arm down quickly.

"Can I come in?" A Benzinni woman walked in through the door, just not the one she was expecting. Charlie got super nervous and tried sitting up to the best of her abilities, putting her good arm up to her forehead in the form of a salute. "At ease, Officer Reigns, please."

Charlie smiled the best she could, she was nervous to a point she felt like her shaking was making the bed shake. Not only was she the New York City Police Commissioner, but she was, most importantly, Allison's mother.

"I don't want to disturb you any more than I have to. I just wanted to make sure you were doing okay" She looked back at the empty chair behind her and then back at that girl she had heard so many good things about. "May I sit?"

"Yes, of course," Charlie cleared her throat nervously. "Ma'am, yes, of course, Ma'am."

"So, how are you doing?"

"I'm in a bit of pain, but nothing that the morphine isn't taking care of," She tried joking around and was relieved when Claudia laughed.

"I've heard your performance tonight was amazing, Officer Reigns, and I would like to thank you and congratulate you for that. I can imagine it was hard, and you must have been tired after a long day of work, so thank you very much for your service" Claudia smiled. Truthfully, she had had a bigger hand in making Officer Reigns her daughter's T.O. than any of her children knew. She was one of the best female officers in the city, and even though she had reservations about two female officers being paired together, she knew Charlie was the one to make her daughter into the best police officer she could be.

"That's okay, Ma'am. I was just doing my job."

"I would also like to thank you for taking such good care of my daughter and teaching her so well, Officer Reigns. You are an amazing addition to the New York City Police Department, and I'll make sure your performance tonight gets rewarded" Before Charlie could answer her, Allison barged in ready to say something but stopped as quickly as she had come in when she saw her Mom sitting down beside Charlie.

"Emm, Mom?" She looked terribly confused for a few seconds until she seemed to remember that her Mom was the police commissioner and Charlie was an injured police officer.

"Where are your manners, Allison? You knock before going through a closed door," Claudia herself forgot for a second where she was and who she was while she reprimanded her daughter for her behavior.

"That's okay, Commissioner. I texted your daughter a few minutes back before you arrived, telling her my room number," Charlie tried to help her friend out, but that made it even worse.

"It's not okay, Officer Reigns. A knock should always be used before entering a closed door."

"Yes, Ma'am," she quickly answered, scared to get onto the commissioner's bad side.

"I was going to leave anyhow" she stood up, looking disappointedly at her daughter before turning around to look at Charlie. "I really hope you have a good and speedy recovery Officer, we are looking forward to having you back at work."

Claudia left, and as soon as she closed the door, Allison lunged herself towards her partner.

"Ouch!" She winced out in pain, and Allison quickly stepped back.

"You idiot, what were you thinking going after that man without back-up or a bulletproof vest, you idiot" she yelled before she started crying her eyes out.

Charlie couldn't help but smile when she saw her. She was falling for Allison Benzinni. Since she had felt her lips, there was no doubt in her mind, but she also knew that it couldn't happen. They would have to stop being partners in order for them to be romantically involved, and that wasn't possible for them.

"I had to, Ali, I couldn't let him get away" Charlie's face saddened, realizing that she hadn't caught him, and Allison was quick to realize what was going through her partner's mind.

"They're going to find him, you gave a really good description, and they basically shut down all of Brooklyn, so please don't worry"

Allison ended up lying in the bed beside Charlie. They fell asleep and only woke up when they heard a knock on the door.

"Come in" Charlie cleared her throat, which was still asleep, and Allison stood up waiting for whoever was on the other side of the door to enter.

"Hi girls, it's just me," Jackson entered with a chart in his hand and smiled when he saw Charlie smile. "I see you're doing great."

"Really tired but great," she joked.

"I'm leaving to go home now, we'll keep you here for a few days to make sure everything is okay, but you seem great."

"Thank you very much," She sincerely said. She could see some similarities between Ali and her older brother. They both had the same crooked smile and the same happy eyes. She couldn't help but smile, looking at the both of them, who were now hugging goodbye.

"If you need anything, just give Mindy or me a call, and we'll be here right away," Allison closed her eyes, feeling the warmth in her brothers hug and smiled.

"I'm sure everything will be okay" Jackson waved goodbye and opened the door. Before he closed it, he turned to the girls smiling, "By the way, amazing work today, I'm glad he was finally caught" he closed the door before the girls could answer back, so they just turned and looked at each other confused.

"Turn on the TV," Charlie asked, turning her full attention to the TV. Allison was quick to turn it on and just at the right time.

"Jonathan Reed, a 47-year-old native New Yorker was apprehended a few minutes ago by officers in downtown Brooklyn, he is suspected of being the shooter in tonight's horrible attacks," The news reporter read as she wore her serious face on the TV

"We have also received news that the injured Officer is stable, conscious and will be going home in the next few days."

Allison and Charlie turned to smile at each other. They looked at each other intensely, they were both looking for answers in each other's eyes, but they didn't get any that night.

7 THIS IS WRONG

It was a really early morning for Allison that 24th of November, but she was so excited to be back to working with Charlie after three weeks that she didn't even mind that her nieces were running around naked, not giving in to being dressed for school.

"Girls, I'm going to count until three. If you're not with Aunt Allison getting changed, you don't get your iPads," Eve started counting from the bathroom where she was putting Alex's hair in a braid.

The girls took half a second to get to their aunt, and they were dressed and ready in no time. While they were having breakfast, Eve and Allison sat on the sofa, drinking their cups of coffee while having a quick chat.

"How are you doing?" Allison asked, looking for a sincere answer from her sister-in-law, who she could see was extremely tired yet still looking incredibly beautiful.

"I'm tired," she laughed with sad eyes, "And I miss your brother too much, but I'm getting through it."

"I think you're the strongest person in the world," Allison said sincerely, looking at those three little, really cute monsters having breakfast.

"I'm making it work, which is enough," she looked over at the clock on the wall and got up quickly. "We're late, everyone shoes on and into the car."

"Do you want me to drive them to school, Eve?" Allison asked, seeing how stressed Eve had become in a few seconds.

"I thought Charlotte was picking you up here."

"She is, but I'm sure she would have no problem getting us to the school."

Eve ended up saying yes, and Charlie wanted to kill her partner when she saw her standing on the doorstep with three children's seats ready to be placed in her car.

"Charlie," Alex screamed, running into her arms. Charlie hugged her tightly, giving her a kiss on the forehead followed by a hug from each one of the twins.

"I'm so sorry," Ali whispered, leaving a quick kiss on her cheek while taking the car seats into the backseats.

They ended up being late, but as it was Charlie's first shift back, she was excused. They had been driving around in silence for a few minutes waiting for a call to come in.

"I missed you," Allison said sincerely, looking at her partner, who was very focused while driving down the busy streets.

"You've come over to my house every single day, Benzinni," she laughed with that beautiful smile that made Allison go crazy. "You couldn't have possibly missed me."

"You're saying it like you didn't want me to go over every single day," she pretended to be offended, which only caused Charlie to laugh even more.

"I never said that."

"Oh Allison, I'm bored to death. Please come and watch *Friends* with me… please, I'm begging," Allison pretended to be Charlie calling her basically every single day of her leave.

She received a soft slap from her when they reached a red light.

"You're so funny," Charlie pretended to laugh but quickly turned her smile into a frown making Allison burst into tears laughing.

They answered a few minor calls, and anyone who saw them could see they were really happy to be working back together after almost a month apart. But that happiness was soon going to be transformed by a really disturbing call.

"All units, 10-13. We have received a distressed call from a very young child. Screams for help could be heard in the background. Please wait for confirmation on the location" They both went dead quiet, waiting for the location to come through so they could help the child as fast as possible. "Location confirmed. 2161 Madison Ave Bridge. Apartment Building 3B. Approach with caution."

Allison turned on the lights and sirens, and they blasted through the traffic. It didn't take them more than two minutes to arrive. They ran out of the car and up the stairs, guns drawn, and approached apartment 3B with extreme caution. They gave their location through the radio, so dispatch knew they were at the scene.

"NEW YORK POLICE DEPARTMENT. OPEN THE DOOR!" Charlie banged on the door a few times, but the dead silence they were answered with scared both of them. They kicked the door in and were petrified with the scene in front of them.

Allison looked at Charlie and received Charlie's eyes with the same sadness hers had. They looked back at the scene in front of them. A girl not older than five years old was sitting in a puddle of blood weeping, to each side of her were two dead bodies. A man's and a woman's.

Charlie put her gun away and started walking forward with the intention of picking up the kid, but Allison stopped her, grabbing her arm.

"We should search the apartment first, Charlie," she whispered without taking her eyes off the little girl cleaning her tears away with her blood-filled hands.

"I'm going to pick that kid up first, Allison, and make sure she's not hurt."

"Charlie," she stopped her again, "She doesn't seem hurt or in pain. I think you should wait for the detectives."

"Officer Benzinni," Charlie turned to face Allison for the first time. Her face was serious. "I'm going to pick this child up, clear the apartment."

"Yes, Officer Reigns." She answered angrily and started searching the apartment, which was fully cleared.

When she returned, there were many officers entering the apartment, Charlie sat on a chair, holding the little girl tightly. Allison got closer and could hear how she whispered a song to the girl while soothing her.

"The apartment is cleared, Officer Reigns" Charlie looked up to her, and Allison could see how she felt bad for the way she had talked to her before, but she also knew Charlie wouldn't be apologizing.

"Your sister and her partner have gotten the case. They should be here at any moment, go downstairs and make sure to brief them about everything" She answered harsher than Allison would have expected, which made her a little angry.

"Should I also tell them the part where you picked up the girl even though I told you not to?"

"You tell them whatever you think is important in the case, Officer Benzinni, now listen to my orders before I have to write you up" Allison turned around, angry, very angry at Charlie's way of speaking to her.

She ran down the stairs trying to relieve her anger, but before she could go outside to breathe a bit of fresh air, she saw Ellie and her partner Tom walking into the building, followed by Sergeant Wells.

"Allison," her sister called out to her, and Ali put on her best smile to receive them.

"Hi, so you want me to walk you through it?" Ellie nodded, and Allison briefed them while they walked up the stairs.

"Officer Reigns decided to pick the girl up to inspect for injuries, and I finished searching the apartment, and then everyone else arrived," She concluded when they reached the door.

As soon as they reached the apartment, all their heads turned to the gruesome image in front of them.

"Okay, well, I think the best thing right now is to have all your officers clear the scene, Sergeant Wells," Ellie spoke, and that is what Sergeant Wells started doing.

"Has social services been notified?" Tom asked Allison while still looking at Charlie, who walked around the apartment corridor with the girl holding onto her tightly.

"Yes, they shouldn't take long," Allison answered, not taking her eyes off her partner.

"Okay, so Detective Benzinni, I'm leaving two of my men on the door to watch. Everyone else is clearing out," Ellie smiled at her and turned to look at Tom.

The woman from social services arrived. She spoke to Ellie, and then the two of them walked to Charlie, followed by Maria and Allison.

"Okay, I'm sure you all have a lot of work to do, so I'll take it from here," The woman stretched her arms out to pick the girl up, but Charlie didn't make any movements.

"Officer Reigns, please give the girl to Miss Carpenter so you can get changed and get back to your shift," Maria spoke carefully, but Charlie still held onto the girl tightly, and the girl held onto her. "Officer Reigns, that is an order."

"Officer Reigns," Allison now whispered. Charlie looked up at her. She saw Charlie's saddened eyes, and Ali quickly turned to look at her sister. She gave her a stare, and Ellie knew her sister enough to know what she wanted from her.

"Sergeant Wells, actually, if you didn't mind, I'd appreciate Officer Reigns and Officer Benzinni's help with this." Ellie tried her best to not undermine the sergeant's orders but still help her sister.

"No problem, but Officer Reigns, please come to my office when you've finished your shift so we can have a chat." Sergeant Wells left, and Charlie stayed with the social service woman while Ellie and Allison walked back to the crime scene.

"We're going to talk about this later."

Allison nodded before helping out however she could while keeping an eye on Charlie, who had just passed the girl to the woman.

"What happens with her now?" Charlie asked the woman, who looked at her kindly.

"We'll search to see if she has any relatives who can take care of her and if not, she will go into the system, but even if she does with her age, she'll probably get adopted really easily."

"Have you found out her name yet?" She asked, caressing the sleepy girl's back and staring at her with adoration.

"Rose White."

Charlie stared at the little blue-eyed girl. She couldn't help but think what that little girl could have done to deserve that beginning in life.

"But I do need to take her now, Officer Reigns."

"Yes, of course," she apologized with a faint smile. "Is there any way I could get a phone number or give you mine so you can let me know if you find family or to let me know what happens with her"

"I'm not supposed to, but if you give me your number I'll give you a call when I know what will happen with her" They exchanged numbers, and soon enough, she left with a crying Rose in her arms.

Allison couldn't help but look at Charlie, who was resting on the window frame looking out into the street.

"Hey Ellie, do you need any help here, or can we be done for today?" Ellie looked over at her sister's partner and then turned back to her sister.

"You can leave but make sure she goes to speak with her sergeant as soon as she's finished with her shift." Ali smiled and turned around to go and get Charlie, but she turned around before being too far away.

"Ellie," she called, and Ellie apologized to the forensic team she was working with and turned around. "Thank you" Her sister smiled at her, and she headed towards Charlie.

"Hey Char, we can leave now," She put her hand on her friend's shoulder, but Charlie was quick to brush her off.

"When we get to the precinct, we have to have a conversation," And with that, she headed out not without stopping to thank Ellie for her help before walking down the steps.

They didn't take long to get to the precinct. Allison waited for

Charlie to finish her conversation with Maria, which was filled with screaming but ended up in a calm hug, so she took that it had ended well. When she was out, they headed into the lockers, and after having changed, they walked out together like they always did, except this time they walked two meters separated and without a single word being shared.

"Allison, I'm your training officer and your superior," She started when they sat down on a bench near the precinct entrance. "When we are on the streets, you do as I say, and you most definitely don't tell me what I can or can't do. If you believe I've acted wrongly, you write me up to Maria." Allison was taken aback, and Charlie felt it and felt bad, so she sat closer to her and took her hand into hers. "We are friends, Allison, but out in those streets, I am in charge and responsible for you, so you can't second guess my actions or decisions. If you are not sure of the nature of my actions, you ask me when we are back in the squad or at the precinct" Charlie took a big breath and felt terrible when she saw Allison's teary eyes, but as her teacher, she needs her to have a few boundaries. "Is it clear, Allison?"

"Crystal, Officer Reigns."

8 I'M SORRY

Allison felt chills all over her body as she got to the door of her childhood home, the Christmas weather was biting hard, and she was freezing. She pulled her keys out of her bag, and as soon as she went into the house, she was greeted by all her nieces and nephews. She took her time to play with them before joining the cooking chores with the adults.

She was dreading the moment where she was alone with Ellie, so she avoided it as much as she could, but when it came time to have dessert, Ellie was quick to offer them both to serve it.

"No, Dad please, Ali and I will bring the dessert out." Allison bit her lip as she followed her older sister into the kitchen. She trembled when Ellie closed the door behind them.

"What do you want me to carry?" She pretended, hoping that the fact that Ellie had offered them to go together didn't mean she wanted to talk.

"Cut the crap. What is going on between Charlotte and you?" She was direct, and Ali was definitely not expecting that.

"What? Nothing."

"Okay, well, if nothing is going on yet, are you ready to admit to me that you're falling head over heels for your training officer?"

"Ellie, I'm not" She couldn't confess anything. She wanted to, she wanted to trust her older sister, but she didn't know who was asking if her older sister or a detective above her in the department.

"I'm not asking as your superior, Allison," She said as if she had read her mind. "I'm not going to tell Mom or dad, I'm not going to tell your Sergeant, but I need to know if what you are feeling can compromise your work and put your partner and you in danger."

"What I feel won't put us in danger. I'm not acting on it. We aren't acting on it." she tried to reassure Ellie the best she could, but she could tell by the way her sister was looking at her that she didn't believe a word that was coming out of her mouth.

"Have you kissed?" Allison saw Ellie's face and could already tell her sister was making things up in her mind and didn't need an answer. The redness that had crept into her cheeks was all the answer she needed. "You have to be careful Allison, you know that couples working together never end well."

"We haven't kissed."

"Oh, come on, you looked like Olivia when I asked her who gave her the chocolates on Valentine's Day." That made Allison laugh and release some of the tension she had been carrying around, but she looked at Ellie with nothing but seriousness on her face.

"We haven't kissed. We haven't expressed any kind of romantic feeling for each other. If I ever feel like our feelings could compromise our work together, I will ask for another partner. I promise."

"I just don't want you to get hurt Allison, once you've fallen for your partner when a bullet is on its way to their chest, you don't think twice before jumping in between that bullet and its destination."

"You'd jump in front of a bullet for me?" Allison laughed, hoping her sister wouldn't say no.

"Of course I would, which is why we couldn't work together either." before she could finish, Jamie walked into the kitchen with a smile on his face.

"I mean, we knew you guys wanted to have a chat when you offered to bring the dessert, but we've been waiting for five minutes" Allison shuffled her nephew's hair before picking up the plates and heading out.

They had a good afternoon, but it didn't take long for Allison to have to leave for her night shift. Charlie picked her up at her house, and they both made their way to the precinct. The incident a few weeks back was already forgotten by both of them. It had made them a bit uneasy the first few shifts after it had happened, but they both decided to put it behind them.

"Can I drive today?" Allison never drove, Charlie liked being in charge of the wheel, but when she looked at her so cheerful, begging to be behind the wheel, she couldn't say no. "Really?" She squealed when Charlie showed her the car keys. She ran towards her, taking the keys and hugging her in the process.

"Please don't kill us," Charlie said, putting on her seatbelt tightly.

"I'm an amazing driver, just for your information." And she wasn't bad. They talked like they hadn't talked in a long time. They laughed, sang, and joked to each other continuously. Allison couldn't stop thinking how she'd love her life to be beside that woman, and she got scared, scared that she was starting to feel too much for Charlie.

"Be advised we're receiving a 10-52 domestic disturbance 190 West-End avenue apartment 1C" Dispatch talked through the radio, and they were quick to answer.

They got to the building fairly quickly, and when they arrived at apartment 1C, the door was open, so they entered carefully.

"Police. HANDS UP!" Charlie shouted, drawing her gun as they walked in on a big man beating a woman to death on the floor. "This is Officer Reigns requesting immediate back up at 190 West-End Avenue."

"STOP RIGHT NOW!" The situation was really tense, the man

wouldn't stop, and Charlie and Allison were running out of options. "Tase him, Charlie."

Charlie did as Allison suggested, she put her gun back in its place and took the taser, gun, shooting the man right in the back, but it didn't work.

"Charlie, he's going to kill her!" Allison's voice was terrified. She didn't know how to help, she didn't want to shoot him.

"STOP! HANDS UP, OR I'LL SHOOT!" Charlie repeated that same sentence twice, but the man wouldn't stop, so she did what she didn't want Allison to have to do. One of them had to.

Time went slowed. Allison's face turned to look at Charlie, not knowing what to do. As she did, she saw Charlie starting to push her finger down on the trigger. She was going to shoot. Everything went really slow yet really quickly at the same time.

"She shot two times, Officer Reigns tried to stop the bleeding while I tried to help the woman, and that's it. He didn't make it. She did. We had no other options, he was going to kill her." Hours had gone by since the shooting. Both Allison and Charlie were in questioning, but it had been a clean shot. Charlie was going to be cleared quickly.

"Okay, Officer Benzinni, that will be all, thank you" The IA agent let her go, and she quickly left the room hoping to find Charlie somewhere. She hadn't been able to talk to her. After the shooting, they had separated them so they couldn't talk, but she needed to make sure she was okay. She looked around the precinct but couldn't find her. The only person she saw was Ellie, who was talking to the IA agent with who she had been talking with minutes ago.

She called her over, and Ellie excused herself with the agent and walked over to her sister, hugging her.

"Hey, are you okay?" Ellie asked worried, she had killed someone before, and even if they were bad people, it was hard to get around the first kill, really hard.

"Yeah, I'm fine. It's Charlie I'm worried about."

"It was a clean shoot. As soon as the psychologist clears her, she will be back" Ellie tried to paint a nicer picture than it actually was, but she knew that Allison had been there through all of the family's first kills, and she knew they were hard.

"I know she'll be cleared, and you know that's not what I'm worried about" Allison still looked around every time she heard a door close or open, hoping that Charlie would come out, but she didn't know where she was.

"All you can do for her is be by her side and make sure that she knows she did the right thing."

"Hey, did you come for me, or do you have another case?"

"I have another case, but I heard and wanted to talk to the IA agent."

"In that case, if you don't mind, I'm going to head to Charlie's house to see if she's gone there cause I can't find her anywhere," she hugged her sister, thanking her for her help and headed to the lockers to change quickly before catching a cab to Charlie's apartment.

Allison walked up the stairs to Charlie's first-floor apartment. She got to her door, but before knocking, she stopped herself after hearing a sob coming from inside. She couldn't help but feel bad. It could have been her to shoot instead of Charlie. She froze, she didn't shoot. Charlie had to.

She knocked softly, not wanting to startle her.

"Who is it?" Charlie's broken voice made her way to Allison's ears, and she immediately felt like crying.

"It's me, Char" the door opened slowly and revealed a tear-stained Charlie with red puffy eyes.

As soon as the door was closed, Charlie clung to Allison, who held her tightly, letting Charlie break down in her arms. They spent close to an hour just sitting on the sofa, Allison sitting upright and Charlie hugging onto her crying.

"Char, are you okay?" Allison was starting to get worried. She hadn't seen much of that 'broken' Charlie, her Charlie was always happy and okay.

"No," she whispered. She calmed herself down and breathed deeply. "I… I killed someone, Allison."

"You killed someone who was trying to kill someone else, Charlie. If you hadn't shot him, she would be dead right now."

"I know, but maybe we could have done something else, something to save them both" she was so sad, it was killing Allison.

"We tried to tase him, Charlie. He was too big. We couldn't deal with him quickly enough to save her," Charlie finally fell out of their hug and cleaned her eyes with the back of her hands.

"We did what we had to do," she whispered.

"Yes, baby, that's exactly what we did."

Their eyes met, Charlie's bright blue eyes shined with tears and Allison's brown ones shined with anticipation of what was going to happen. They were both going to feel that thing they had been longing for since it had happened last.

Allison was the one to take the lead. Her thumb brushed away some of the tears that had made their way to Charlie's lips. Charlie trembled at the touch on her lower lip. Her eyes slowly fell on Allison's lips. They were going to kiss. Allison moved her hand back, now pulling some dangling hairs behind Charlie's ear. They were going to kiss. Ali's gravity pulled her towards Charlie. They were close, close enough for them to be breathing each other in.

"Allison, I - " Charlie pulled back, running her hands through her hair. "I'm sorry, I want, we can't do this" she stood up and started running back and forth, trying to think clearly.

"Charlie, I'm sorry, I - " Now Allison was starting to panic. This was the first time they actually acknowledged that they were going to kiss. It was the first time they'd demonstrated to each other that there were feelings, really confusing feelings, but feelings never the less.

"I'm going to go."

"Allison, don't. I just, we can't."

"Please, just, I need to leave," and she did without another word.

As Allison left, she heard a frustrated, muffled scream come from Charlie, along with the pounding of her fist on the bed. Allison tried not to cry on her way to her apartment. She showered, trying to get rid of all the unwanted feelings that were stuck to her mind and skin. She rubbed her lips especially hard, hoping to eliminate the need they had to touch Charlie's.

The phone caught her off guard, and she nearly tripped trying to get it.

"Yes?" She answered without looking at the caller id.

"Aunt Ali," Olivia's sweet voice through the phone made her smile, "I won!"

"What did you win?" she replied as enthusiastically as the news had been delivered to her.

"A photography contest and it was for the whole state."

"Wow," she exaggerated her happiness for her niece, "I didn't know you had entered, congratulations little winner."

"Mom wants you all to come over for dinner tonight to celebrate. Will you come?" All Allison wanted to do was to lie in bed and scream at herself for a few hours before falling asleep, but she knew how disappointed Olivia would be, so she put on a smile and said yes.

She didn't take long to get dressed and head to her sister's house. And it took even less for the whole family to be seated at the table devouring five pizzas.

"Are you kidding me? A ceremony and everything?" Richard asked her granddaughter, who showed the picture with which she had won proudly.

"Yes, and I have to give a speech."

"Practice here," Alex asked her, and Olivia being the social butterfly she was smiled and got ready to deliver her speech.

"The photograph that made me win is a photo of my Uncle Parker. My uncle passed away a few months ago, but he is still very alive in every one of our hearts. I loved him a lot, and I know one of the things he always said to me was that love is the greatest magic in the world and to never let any kind of love get away from you, so to anyone in this room who hasn't said I love you to their special people, do it now."

Allison couldn't help but feel that those words which had just come out of her niece's mouth were directed to her even if she knew it wasn't possible. She didn't remember Parker ever saying that. It sounded too emotional for him, but he supposed it would have been one of the things he said to Olivia when his dad died.

The rest of the family clapped as the little one stood on the chair, accepting the claps gracefully. But Allison's mind went a hundred miles an hour.

"That was beautiful, Olivia," Allison smiled, standing up. "But I just remembered I had something really important to do, so I'll see you guys later." After a quick round of kisses, Allison ran out of the house and made her way to an apartment building but not hers. She had gone to set things straight with Charlie. She needed to.

9 WHY NOT?

Allison knocked after having spent ten minutes replaying in her head what she was going to say to Charlie. She was close to leaving a few times but decided that if she didn't say it that day, she would never say it.

When she didn't answer the first knock, she turned around. Maybe it was a sign from the heavens above? But her own brain made her turn around again and knock for a second time but louder. There was no answer then either. She was about to leave when the door opened, revealing a rather tall, curvy brown-haired woman with her naked body wrapped around with a blue towel that she knew was Charlie's.

Allison was shocked, to say the least. Confusion was written all over her face. She couldn't wrap her mind around the fact that a naked woman had opened Charlie's door hours after having left there because they were about to kiss.

"I'm so sorry I must have gotten the wrong apartment," she prepared to leave, but the girl laughing caught her off guard.

"By the look on your face, you must be the girl my sister is crazy about" Allison stood dead still. She didn't even move a finger. "Don't worry, I won't tell her how jealous you looked."

"I didn't... I, you're Charlie's sister?

"The one and only," She stared her up and down but couldn't find any similarities between the both. They were completely contrary.

"I didn't know she had a sister," She said truthfully. It had never come up in conversation.

"She doesn't like talking about family because of all the abandonment issues" By Allison's estranged face, Charlie's sister could tell she had screwed up. "Please forget I just said that I… the way she talked about your relationship, I thought you knew, but I should have guessed with all the you not knowing of my existence and all."

It took a few seconds for Allison to acknowledge what she had heard, but she had no idea what this girl in front of her was saying. What abandonment issues?

"I won't say anything. Emm, sorry, what's your name?"

"I'm Rachel." They didn't hug. Allison didn't even move. She was really confused.

"Emm, I'm Allison, but I think you know that."

"I do," she smiled, and even though they looked nothing alike, Allison could see some of Charlie's mannerisms in the girl. "My sister went to get some takeout. You can come in and join us. I'm sure she wouldn't mind."

"No, no, I just, I was going to…." But she didn't know what to say, she couldn't tell the truth. "I need to get going. I was just going to drop something off."

Allison realized that Rachel Reigns had seen she was carrying nothing in her hands, but Rachel had also realized Allison was expecting to find her sister opening that door, so she opted on giving her an easy way out and not insisting.

"Yeah, of course, well, it was really great meeting you." They hugged goodbye, and Allison was quick to leave. She headed to her house and had a difficult time going to sleep with everything that had happened.

The morning came too quickly for her. She hid under the covers when her alarm clock blasted on her bedside table. It was too early. After snoozing the phone for about 20 minutes, she had to end up running to not be late.

"Hey," Charlie smiled when she saw her walk into the locker room.

"Good morning." their smiles were sincere. They were both confused and what had happened the day before had them both questioning a lot about their relationship.

"Rachel told me you came by last night. I'm sorry for anything she could have said."

"That's okay, she was extremely nice."

"She's an extremely nice person,"

Allison smiled, seeing how proud she seemed of her sister.

"She looks absolutely nothing like you."

"Yeah, it'd be weird if she did." Allison frowned at that, not really understanding. "She's adopted."

"Okay, that makes so much more sense now" they both laughed, and it seemed like the tension fell much lower than it had been just seconds before.

"I didn't know you had a sister," Charlie couldn't help but realize that she had heard a bit of hurt in that, and she felt bad.

"I don't really enjoy talking about family."

"Yeah, I see."

"Hey girls, roll-call is starting." They left their conversation and headed into a long day of work.

"Hey, how come you came to my apartment?" Allison was hoping she wouldn't ask because she didn't want to lie, but after having

82

met her adopted sister, she realized she knew nothing about this girl that was sitting beside her in the car.

"I was just going to drop off some leftover carrot cake I had made."

"You went all the way from your house to mine just to give me a piece of carrot cake?"

"Emm… Yes?" Charlie laughed at the fact that her answer was more of a question, Allison knew she didn't believe a word she said, but she could imagine what Allison wanted to say, and she thought it was best for her not to hear it.

"And why didn't you bring it to me today?"

"I… I ate it?"

Charlie laughed it off and decided not to continue questioning her, but Allison wanted to try and get something out of her.

"Charlie?" Her voice was soft, and Charlie immediately knew she wanted something.

"Yes?" She faced her when they reached the red light.

"Why haven't you ever talked to me about your family?" It wasn't that she didn't trust her. Charlie probably trusted Allison more than anyone else in the world. It was just something she didn't talk about. She never did.

"It's not because I don't trust you or anything like that," Charlie turned her attention to the road when the light turned green. "I just, I've never really spoken of it to anyone."

"It's okay, you don't have to tell me," Allison placed her hand on Charlie's, which was resting on her leg. "I'm sorry for even asking."

"No, I'll tell you, it's okay," Charlie turned her hand around, holding Allisons as she put the car in park in a near street. "My parents put me into ballet since I was a midget, I was good, really good, but it wasn't my dream. I wanted to be a police officer like my brother."

"You also have a brother," Allison was a bit shocked. She talked so much about her family and especially her siblings that it was weird for her when other people didn't do the same.

"Had. He died nearly nine years ago on duty." As she heard that, Allison held her hand tighter and now turned her whole body to face Charlie.

"Char, I'm so sorry."

"It's okay," she smiled. "I always wanted to be like him, but my parents insisted on me doing ballet, so I continued training until I was around seventeen. I received a scholarship to Juilliard, but I turned it down to go to the police academy."

Allison noticed Charlie's body suddenly become extremely tense.

"Hey," she let go of her hand and softly caressed her arm, "It's okay, stop."

"No, no, I'm finishing anyways" she turned to look at Allison, and they smiled at each other when their eyes met. "Because of my brother dying while on the job, they didn't want me going to the academy, they wanted me to go to Juilliard and dance, but I decided on the police academy, and they gave me an ultimatum." Her face turned into a sad frown, and Allison felt horrible for having asked in the first place. "They said if I went to the police academy, they would kick me out of the house, and they did."

"But...Charlie that is horrible. I... I had no idea. I'm so sorry" Allison tried to hug her the best she could, but between the small space they had in their car and their uniforms, it was a really awkward hug.

"It's okay, that's why Rachel had come over. We celebrate an early Christmas dinner."

"You're alone on Christmas?"

"*Nope*," she now smiled, "You and I will be working until 6pm, and then I'll go home, watch a nice Christmas movie, and I'll be in bed ready for work the next day."

"Come and have dinner with us," Allison didn't really think about what she had said. No one who wasn't "officially" part of the family had ever come to a Christmas dinner, not even a regular family dinner.

"No way," Ali saw how Charlie suddenly got nervous and laughed. "A table full of Benzinni's and the police commissioner, I'd rather have dinner alone, thank you very much."

"Hey," they joked around a bit, and their shift finished after a few minor calls. They each went home that day worried that if they shared a moment alone out of work, the inevitable would happen.

10 FINALLY

Charlie

It was way too early when the phone ringing woke Charlotte up. She and Allison had spent the whole night awake watching Christmas movies and eating chocolate even though Christmas was already over. Allison had just left an hour before that phone call was waking her up.

"Yeah, what? I'm up," she mumbled over the phone. When she heard laughing over the other line, she quickly took her phone off her ear and looked at the caller id. She didn't have the number saved. "Sorry, who is this?"

"Officer Reigns, glad to see my sister and you had fun last night."

"Detective Benzinni?" Charlie couldn't help but panic. Why in the world was Allison's sister calling her so early in the morning.

"Officer Reigns, I need you in my precinct as soon as possible."

"I… Did something happen?" She didn't know if her confusion was a mixture of tiredness and Ellie calling or if what was happening really didn't make any sense.

"We need your help on a case, Charlotte, if you don't mind me calling you that."

"No, no, of course, Charlie, Charlotte, Officer Reigns, whatever you like is perfect with me" Ellie couldn't help but find the young officer amusing. Not only had she managed to make her sister fall head over heels, but she seemed like a genuinely good officer.

"We need you here as soon as possible, and please don't say a word to anyone."

They hung up, and Charlie started getting ready, she had a shower to wake herself up, and in twenty minutes, she was on her way to Ellie's precinct. When she got there, Ellie and her partner Tom were ready to greet her.

"I'm so sorry for not letting you sleep. I know my sister was at your house until early this morning" By Ellie's face, Charlie realized what she was either implying or just thought had happened.

"I, Ellie, Detective Benzinni. Allison and I are just friends," she said it so quickly that even Tom couldn't help but chuckle.

"Calm down, Reigns. My sister tells me everything. I know you guys were watching movies."

"Oh yeah, of course," The three of them went into the precinct, and they were escorted to an office on the fourth floor. When Tom opened the door, there were two men inside wearing black suits. Even though they didn't really know each other, Charlie looked for answers in Ellie by turning her body towards her and making herself small.

"Officer Reigns, this is Agent Johnson and Agent Lopez from the FBI," Ellie tried to make her feel comfortable when she saw her so young and fragile by sitting close to her and not on the other side of the table as was intended.

"Officer Reigns, you aren't in any trouble." Charlie breathed deeply, and they all laughed with her at her relief.

"My name is George, and this is Manuel. We have been investigating this case over the last year" A few folders were placed and opened in front of Charlie, revealing some photos of different women, empty houses, and a few pictures of horrifying-looking men. "The last six months, Spanish prostitutes residing in America have been getting kidnapped and flown to Russia. We need an undercover agent to help us take this down from the inside. We need the big guns running all these operations, not the men who just transport."

"And you want me to be your undercover girl?"

"You fit the description, aside from your blonde hair, which we would have to change. You're really young, you speak Spanish fluently, and you have the experience." Ellie was the one to answer her now. She saw how nervous the girl had become, so she placed her hand gently on her arm.

"I have experience, but I've never done anything like this," Charlie suddenly felt little. She wasn't sure if she'd be ready.

"If you're up for the challenge, you'll have time to prepare, you'll be in your normal shifts, for now, to not raise any suspicions, and in the afternoons, you'll work with detective Benzinni to get everything clear and for you to feel ready and safe" Agent Lopez now explained, they were all looking at her which made her uneasy.

"You don't have to do it, Officer Reigns," Ellie was kind of hoping she would say no. She knew when her sister found out she would want to kill her. She didn't know if Allison would forgive her if something bad happened to Charlotte in the operation.

"I want to. If you can help me get ready, I'll be ready." She was eager, and everyone in the room liked that.

That morning Ellie worked with Charlotte for hours on end. They went over her backstory, what she would have to do, what had happened with the girls. They left everything clear that day. When they finished, it was already nighttime.

"I bet you can't wait to get home and see your little one," Allison talked about her family a lot. Due to that, Charlie probably knew much more about Ellie than Ellie knew about her.

"She'll probably be asleep when I get home, but I'll spend the day with her tomorrow when she comes back from school" Ellie couldn't help but smile, thinking about her daughter. Olivia was the love of her life, she was her everything, and Ellie questioned quitting the job she loved every other day because of her. When her husband had died, she thought she wouldn't be able to do it. She wouldn't be able to give Olivia a good childhood while still working, but she made it work. Olivia was an incredibly clever and happy girl who loved spending time with her cousins and grandparents. "How about you? Do you have any plans before going to bed?"

"I was meant to meet up with your sister, but I think I'm going to cancel because I'm too tired" Ellie couldn't help but smile, looking at Charlie's face when she thought about Allison. They were in love, and she knew it better than they knew it themselves.

"Hey Charlie, I do need to remind you that no one can know about this, not even Allison."

"I know, I wasn't going to tell her," Charlie wasn't completely sincere. Her first thought had been that it wouldn't matter if Allison knew. She wasn't going to tell anyone.

"Yeah, I don't 100% believe that" Ellie turned to face Charlie directly. "I don't like keeping my sister in the dark any more than you do, but it's really important that no one, absolutely no one, knows about this."

"Don't worry, I promise I won't tell her."

"I'm really sorry for putting this in between you guys, but I can't express how important it is that this stays between the five people that were in that room this morning."

They ended their day with a hug, and they each went their own way. For about a week, they kept up their timetable, Charlie would go to work for her morning shifts, she would have lunch with Allison to not raise any suspicions, and at 4pm, she'd make her way to Ellie's office to work with Tom and her on the case.

She had one more week before her undercover work would start, and she couldn't wait any longer because lying to Allison was taking every ounce of energy out of her.

"Hey Al, I'm not going to be working for the next few weeks starting Friday, so Wells will assign you a temporary T.O." She tried to make it sound the least suspicious possible as she made a left turn trying to get to the place they had received a possible domestic.

"What? What do you mean?" Allison was so confused. A few weeks off? Charlie?

"I'm taking a personal leave," They arrived at the scene, but that didn't stop Allison from trying to figure out what was going on.

"What do you need a personal leave for?" She whispered as they entered the building.

They heard the shouting from the entrance, and that made them stop their conversation quickly.

"It's in apartment 4A. They're going to kill each other," an elderly woman who had just made her way down the stairs informed them. "You better hurry."

"Ma'am, please go back into your apartment," Allison said before following Charlie up the stairs. "Charlie, what are you taking a personal leave for?"

"This is not the time Benzinni, I want all your attention on what we're doing now."

They got to the apartment and banged on the door loudly.

"NYPD, open up the door!"

The shouting ceased, and a few seconds later, a strong man opened the door, his face was red, and his veins were visible all over his arms, he was really angry.

"What do you want?" He answered in a bad manner. Behind him, a petite woman stood crying.

"Sir, we have received some noise complaints from your neighbors who are worried something might be going on here," Charlie explained as calmly as possible, trying not to provoke the man any further.

"Well, nothing is going on, my wife and I are having a discussion, and that is it" he was going to close the door on them, but Allison quickly placed her foot so the door couldn't shut.

"Ma'am, are you okay?" The woman nodded, but neither Allison nor Charlie felt like it was okay to leave with her like that. "Can you please step outside for a moment?"

Allison stepped to the side with the woman while Charlie asked the man for some ID.

"Has he hit you?"

"No, of course not, he never would, it's just he gets really angry, and we fight, but I scream too it's just I get nervous and cry, but really everything is okay please leave before you make it worse," Allison felt like she was saying the truth, she didn't have any visible marks on her body which wasn't too covered, so she didn't have reasons to believe she was suffering physical damage, but she couldn't be sure about how her husband was affecting her psychologically. Allison realized she didn't really know what to do at that moment.

"Can you wait for me here, please?" she turned and walked over to Charlie, who was trying to calm the man down. "Do you mind if I talk to you for a second?"

Charlie excused herself with the man, and they moved a little bit further away.

"She says he doesn't hit her, but I'm not sure about the emotional damage he can be causing her, but I don't know what to do now or…." Allison tried to explain herself the best she could, there were rare moments when she felt like a rookie, with so many family members in the force she felt like she knew what to do in every circumstance, but this situation had pulled her a little bit off track.

"Okay, so you can ask her if she needs any help and if she insists that it was just a discussion gotten out of hand and she doesn't want to press any charges, you have to let it go," Charlie smiled, she didn't need to teach Allison very often, and she liked being able to help her.

They left the house fairly quickly after that. Before they left, they saw how the man apologized to the woman. It didn't take long for Allison to return to their conversation after entering the car.

"I'm not forgetting. Why are you taking time off?"

"It's personal, Allison," Charlie hated not being able to tell her. She wanted to tell her, to have her be proud of her and to be there to watch her back when she was undercover, but if Ellie had insisted on her sister not knowing, it must have been for a good cause.

"I don't get it. We tell each other everything. Why the secrets all of a sudden?" She was confused, terribly confused as to why Charlie wouldn't tell her what was going on in her life.

"We keep secrets, Allison." Charlie was referring to a very concrete secret that they both kept from each other, but Allison didn't seem to catch on.

"I don't keep any secrets from you."

"So there's nothing you haven't told me?" Charlie was pissed, at herself, at Allison, at Ellie, and at their stupid and confusing relationship.

"No, you know every stupid detail of my life" She wasn't lying. Allison didn't know what Charlie was referring to. She tended to overshare with her partner anything that happened to her or her family Charlie knew.

"Why did you go to my apartment that day that Rachel was there?" And with that, she shut up, and they ended the shift as quiet as they'd ever had.

"I'm sorry for being so insistent," her small broken voice behind her, while they were changing in the locker room made her feel bad. It was normal that she was confused. In any other circumstance, Allison would know why Charlie would take personal leave if she had to. "Can we please forget about it and go get a beer?"

Charlie couldn't help but agree she didn't have to meet with Ellie until 4 PM. They went to a nearby bar and talked and laughed like they always did when they were together.

"I'm going to go to pee really quickly," Charlie ran off as they laughed at the TikTok they had just seen.

Allison

Right, when she had gone into the bathroom, Charlotte's phone, which was on the table with Allison, started ringing. Ali looked down and couldn't help but be really confused when she saw her sister's name on the phone. Why was Ellie calling Charlie?

"Why the hell are you calling my partner?" Ellie didn't expect Allison to pick up the phone, which really screwed up her plans. She knew this would be bad for them. She wouldn't stop asking now.

"Allison? Oh, I was calling Tom. I must have gotten the wrong number. I'm so sorry," she quickly hung up, hoping that Charlotte could take care of the situation and call her back as soon as possible.

"Why were you talking on my phone?"

"Emm... My sister just called you, isn't that weird?" Allison hadn't believed a word that had come out of Ellie's mouth, and she was now trying to see Charlie's reaction. If they were working together, that would explain so many things.

"And why the hell would you answer my phone?" Charlie wasn't actually bothered. They shared their phones all the time, but she knew that if Ellie had called out of schedule, something had to have come up. "You can't just pick up my phone Allison, no matter who it is."

"Hey Char, I'm sorry, I really didn't mean to get into your privacy. I saw it was my sister and I thought maybe she was trying to reach me. I'm really sorry." Allison didn't expect that reaction. Charlotte never spoke to her like that.

"You've been awfully sorry today," Charlie hated it. She wanted to come clean and just tell her what was happening. "I think we should call it and both go home."

"Charlie, I'm sorry," Allison really did feel bad. She didn't think what she had done was so bad.

"It's okay, but let's just call it," Charlie stood up and hugged Allison. "I love you." she kissed her forehead and left.

That was the first time Charlie had said that not only to Allison but to anyone that wasn't her family, but she had a feeling that Ellie's call wasn't good news and she didn't want to leave without having told Allison how she felt, even if it was in that indirect manner, at least once.

She quickly stepped outside and dialed Ellie.

"I'm so sorry about that."

"Charlie, we're moving the op to tomorrow. Our informant in Russia… He just called, Charlie, they've found the dead bodies of the twelve girls who disappeared."

11 WHAT ARE YOU DOING?

It was Friday dinner at the Benzinni household, a Friday after a really tense week. The tension was still terribly noticeable at the dining table, where Alex Benzinni tried to explain to the best of her capabilities why she hadn't been able to do an exercise in class.

"I wanted to be brave and do the trust fall, but I couldn't. My body didn't let me," The rest of the adults laughed, but Allison looked at her with a sad smile.

"I understand why you didn't do it, Alex." She now turned to look at her older sister, who was sat right in front of her eating some ravioli, "I mean, we can't even trust our own family. Why would you trust some kid in your class?"

"Are you still going on about this?" Ellie was so done with her sister's attitude.

"Kids, why don't you all head to the other room and watch the tv while you finish your lunch" The kids were used to leaving the table when the conversation got too heated for them, so they all stood up and headed to the living room.

"You put my partner undercover and didn't even trust in me, your sister, to tell me." Allison was hurt, hurt that neither Charlie nor Ellie had confided in her enough to tell her what she was going to be doing.

"Allison darling, no one has to tell you anything about your partner's assignments and even less so if they are your superiors. She is your training officer, not your friend. If she has undercover work, she must do it without sharing anything with her co-workers, especially not inferior ones." Richard tried to reason for the sixteenth time with her youngest daughter, but she was as stubborn as her mother.

"She's not only my boss, Dad, she's a good friend, and Ellie told her not to tell me specifically," she answered back to her father. She was so angry that she couldn't even explain it properly.

"If I hadn't specifically told her, I knew she would have told you straight away, Allison, and she really couldn't tell any cops, and there's a really good reason for that, she's okay, and she's safe, and that's all I can say." Ellie couldn't help but feel terrible looking at her sister, who was so torn down and tired from not sleeping well. "She wanted to tell you, Ali. We both did, but we couldn't."

"Well, I found out anyways, so the lying was all for nothing" And with that, she excused herself and left the table to breathe.

Three weeks had gone by, Allison didn't know anything about Charlie except the little information Ellie gave her, telling her that she was safe. Her new training officer was horrible. He was so old and so sweaty. She felt like she was working at a geriatric center all day. She was desperate to see her and know that she really was okay.

She'd been snooping around Ellie's folders, and with what she had gathered with that and the small intel Ellie shared with her, she knew that Charlie was working undercover as a prostitute and had a really realistic brown wig. One night she did something she knew she would really regret, but she couldn't help it. Her plan was just to see her, from afar, to see that she was really okay.

She started driving around places she knew prostitutes frequented, and it didn't take long to see her partner standing on the curb. An up to the shoulder brown wig, a very short crop top that didn't leave much to the imagination, and a short pink skirt. It was her, it was Charlie. Before she knew it, she had started driving up to the meeting point. She knew she shouldn't, she knew it was a mistake, but she couldn't help herself. She needed to talk to her.

Charlie quickly recognized her car, and even though it took her off guard, she quickly reacted and got to the car window before another girl could get there.

"What the hell are you doing?" She was happy and terrified to see her. She didn't understand what she was doing there. She had wished so hard every night on the cold mattresses that it would be over and that she and Allison would be back to their day-to-day that she wasn't even sure if she was seeing things.

"I… I'm sorry, I didn't…."

"Get the fuck out of here!" Charlie stepped back, cursing at the car, pretending the person driving had said something insulting to her. Allison quickly drove off, parking the car behind some dumpsters where she could still see her clearly.

She saw how the man she suspected was her pimp hit her while shouting at her. She couldn't accept that. She turned around to get her gun, but when she was about to leave, Ellie got into her passenger seat yelling.

"What the fuck were you thinking about? Are you insane? Have you gone crazy?" She was so angry. Her sister could have screwed up their whole operation. She could have put her life and Charlie's life in danger. She didn't understand what in the world she could have been thinking.

"I… Ellie, I screwed up," she was crying. She didn't know why she had done that. The need to see Charlie had clouded her thoughts.

"Do you realize how badly you could have screwed up? She's a twenty-two-year-old undercover in an FBI investigation that's really dangerous. You could have blown her cover" Her anger couldn't be contained. How could her sister be so stupid?

"I didn't say anything. Calm down."

"You didn't have to, you idiot," she hit her hard on the arm. "She hasn't seen a familiar face in weeks, and without any notice, her rookie, friend, and the girl that she likes and can't wait to see and hug suddenly arrives, putting her off track. She couldn't have known if you were or weren't part of the operation. She could have really screwed up, Allison."

Allison cried as her sister yelled at her, but she knew she deserved every bit of it. She had done a really dumb thing that could have put Charlie in danger.

"You're lucky I'm finishing my shift, and all I want to do is go and see your niece because I swear I would go to your supervisor and get you suspended." Ellie got out of the car and left Allison feeling defeated.

She looked at Charlie one last time and had to force herself to leave and not go after her. She drove around for a while trying to clear her mind. She got home, had a long shower, and put on her pajamas. When she was about to get into bed, she got a message from an unknown number.

I'm sorry I left without saying anything, when I'm back we'll go to where we went on your first day, and we'll have a serious talk about ourselves but please don't come back to where you saw me today, what I'm doing is really important. DON'T text back. I love you. C xx

Allison went to sleep happy. There it was again, the "I love you." She wasn't sure if she had heard right the last time, but now there was proof, written proof.

She arrived at the precinct the next day as happy as could be, but her face quickly changed when she saw the chaos, everyone was running around, and she instantly knew that something was going on, but the thought it could be about Charlie never even crossed her mind.

She quickly spotted Maria in all the chaos, and she ran over to her.

"Maria, what's wrong? How can I help?"

"Benzinni," Maria turned around to face her, and Allison couldn't help but get a bad feeling when she saw her sergeant's red puffy eyes. She had been crying, "What are you doing here?"

"What do you mean, Sergeant? It's my shift." She was confused, and bad feelings were starting to form around in her mind as she looked around at everyone.

"I know Benzinni, it's just… I would've thought your sister would have called you?"

"María? What do you mean? Has something happened to my mother?"

"No, not the commissioner, Ali, it's…." Right, when she was about to say it, an officer came asking for Allison.

"Officer Benzinni, Detective Benzinni has requested your help at her precinct," Allison turned back around to face Maria

"Finish what you were going to say, please."

"Ali, your sister should tell you."

"Please," she whispered, and Maria felt terrible.

"Charlotte disappeared last night. They can't find her."

When Allison arrived at her sister's precinct, she walked over to her angrily and pushed her, making her fall to the floor. Everyone around them suddenly stopped. Ellie quickly stood up and went to hit Allison, but their Mom's voice made them stop dead in their tracks.

"Detective, Officer, come here right now," Claudia Benzinni was appalled with what she had just seen. The three of them made their way into an office, and she closed the door. "I will not tolerate these actions in any of my officers and less of all in my own daughters."

Allison wasn't even paying attention. She was too frustrated and angry to reason with anything or anyone.

"Why didn't you call me when you found out?" She shouted at her sister as tears fell from her eyes.

"You were just going to get in the way, Allison," Ellie felt so terribly bad for her sister at that moment. The fact that Charlie had gone missing was a really bad sign, especially the timing her disappearance had had, "She disappeared right after she sent you that text" Ellie saw the exact moment her sister's heart broke, if they had found that message, they had probably discovered who she was, and she was probably dead.

"Why exactly was an undercover agent sending texts to an officer Elizabeth?"

"We don't know, Ma'am," She lied, trying to cover what her sister had done the night before.

"If your sister won't tell me the truth, maybe you can tell what was so important that one of my undercover officers broke the rules just to send you a message," Claudia asked angrily, raging with the fact that her daughters were involved and weren't telling her the truth.

"Mom, I don't," Allison couldn't talk. She couldn't bear with herself at that moment and, least of all, confront her mother in the state she was in.

"Well, if you won't try to help me as my daughters," She took out her phone and made a call. Once she was finished, she turned her attention back to her daughters. "Detective Benzinni, please have your partner come and brief me on last night's events." Ellie left the room, and Claudia turned to her youngest daughter "Officer Benzinni, as I can tell this is a personal case for you, make sure your sergeant knows you'll be taking the day off and going home."

"Ma'am, if Officer Reigns is missing, I -"

"It's an order, Officer, if you disobey, you will be suspended until further notice."

Allison left but didn't go home. Claudia sat in an office being briefed by Tom while Ellie stood back.

"And last night at twenty-two hours, she sent a text to Officer Benzinni. That was the last they heard of her. She didn't complete her check-in this morning." Claudia read the text and ran her hands through her grey hair.

"Detective Johns, would you mind stepping outside for a minute?"

"Of course not, Commissioner, I will be right outside," As Tom left the room, Claudia stood up and walked around the room thinking about the correct way to ask her daughter.

"Ellie," She turned and walked to her daughter, who was sitting on the desk watching her mother carefully, trying to figure out what her next move would be. "Does your sister have a romantic relationship with her training officer?"

"No," she was really quick to answer. She didn't want to make this worse for her sister or her partner, who she had gotten to really like the last few weeks. "All I know is that they are friends, good friends who spend a lot of time together, but they are not romantically involved."

"How sure are you off this?"

"100%, Ma'am," she answered truthfully.

"And if I ask you like your mother?" Claudia needed an answer. She needed to know the truth so she could treat this case one way or another, so she could talk to her daughter as a grieving girlfriend or just a hurt and worried friend.

"Mom, I can't tell you more," Ellie couldn't do anything more than she was already doing. "It's not my business nor my place to say anything more. As the detective on the case, I can tell you 100% that Officers Benzinni and Reigns aren't romantically involved at this exact moment."

While that conversation was going on, Allison was in her precinct trying to find stuff out from listening to people's conversations or asking around what people knew, but before she could get anything out of Maria Wells, she was called into the FBI center of operations. There was a black car with tinted windows waiting for her when she walked out of the precinct, and she was in the building in a mere five minutes.

After she passed security, she was put into an interrogation room, and she started to freak out.

"Officer Benzinni, thank you for coming in." A male agent wearing a very formal black suit walked in and sat in front of her on the other side of the table.

"Anything I can do to help, sir."

"What was the reason for you going to see Officer Reigns at her undercover post last night?" He asked rather aggressively, and Allison got a bad feeling.

"What do you mean? I just went because… I needed to see her" her voice trembled. The situation put her on edge, and she was really nervous.

"Who are you working with, Officer Benzinni?"

"What are you talking about?" She was now in shock. He couldn't be insinuating what he was right?"

"We knew they were receiving inside help from an officer, but we never would have imagined it would come from the Commissioner's daughter." Allison didn't believe what he was saying. She thought for a moment that it was all a sick prank. "It's quite genius, to be fair."

"I have no idea what you are talking about" she tried to sound as firm as possible.

"Tell us where Officer Reigns is."

"I would love to know," she shouted as tears ran down her face. They couldn't be serious. "I want my sister to be in here."

"I'll give you one call. You can choose who to waste it on" He left her a phone and left swinging the door shut.

Allison tried to recompose herself as best as she could as she dialed Ellie's phone number.

"Ellie, I need you."

12 HOLD ON

The conversation went on for a while. They asked her everything about their relationship, when they had met, how they had met. They even asked her why they had met.

"What the hell do you mean? Why did we meet?" Allison couldn't deal with their stupid questions any longer. "I'm a fucking rookie, and she is my fucking training officer. I met her the day I started working"

"Why do you think Officer Reigns sent you this text?" A printed-out version of the text she had received the night before was placed in front of her.

"She wanted to make sure I didn't go back there, I guess," She was defeated, angry. All she wanted to do was go home and cry.

"Agent Kalahan, can I have a word with you one second?" A woman had walked into the room, the man stood up, and they talked about something for a few seconds, and he returned to his place in front of her, yet the woman didn't leave, she stayed by the open door.

"Officer Benzinni, when she wrote 'We'll go to where we went on our first day,' what did she mean?"

"I'm guessing she meant the restaurant we went to the first day we met. I'm not sure."

"Where is that restaurant located?" She then realized Charlie had left her a message in that text. She was being kept somewhere close to that restaurant.

"It's just by Hudson River. Oh my god," she cried, realizing she might be alive. Both agents ran out, leaving her in there. "Let me out," she banged on the door multiple times, crying, but no one would answer. "Please let me go look for her."

"Officer Benzinni, please settle down." A new agent came in, and she just cried further.

"Please let me go and find her."

"We have multiple officers all around this city looking for her. We need to ask you a few more questions."

"No, no more questions. You've asked every single stupid question. You've been wasting valuable time, you fucking idiots!" She started banging on the door, and she was soon restrained but two officers.

"We can't figure out why you went to her undercover post knowing that could risk her life, yours, and the whole operation."

"BECAUSE I'M IN LOVE WITH HER!" she shouted and then broke down. As she lifted her face, she saw Ellie standing by the open door.

"Let her go," she instructed the officers, and they did as she said after receiving the okay from their boss. "Let's go and find Charlie."

After talking to the agent, Ellie finally got Allison out of there. Tom was waiting in his squad outside, and the three of them made their way to an abandoned warehouse they had just found near Hudson River.

"Please let her be okay, please," Allison whispered to herself as they got closer.

"Bulletproof vest and gun," Ellie passed them to her as she herself put on her vest. "I know you're really emotional right now, Ali, but you need to be focused, or this could end worse."

When they got to the warehouse, hundreds of officers were already entering the building. When they entered, they were all lost for words. There were a lot of young women stripped down lying on mattresses on floors. While Ellie and Tom tried to help all the girls like the rest of the officers, Allison ran around as fast as she could, looking at all those girls' faces trying to find one.

"Allison, have you found her?" Ellie came back in and ran to her sister, who was looking everywhere like crazy.

"No, she's not here."

"This is huge. Let's look in all the rooms and all the boxes, everywhere."

They started opening doors and finding girls, most alive but some dead. Just when she was starting to lose hope, she opened a rusty door and saw her there on the floor. She was completely naked and half beaten to death, her wig on the floor right beside her.

"Charlie, Oh my god," she cried as she fell to the floor beside her holding her in her arms.

Charlie was alive, she was terribly pale, and her body was filled with cuts and bruises, but she was holding on.

"Hold on, Charlie, please hold on" she kissed her forehead, caressing her hair gently. "SHE'S HERE, ELLIE, SHE'S HERE!"

"Allison," Charlie talked, coughing up blood.

"Shh, don't lose energy," she held her to her chest, holding her as tight as she could.

"I love you, Al," but before she could finish, she stopped breathing.

"No, no," Allison put her on the floor and started doing CPR on her. "Please, please. HELP, I NEED HELP!"

The ambulance arrived, and they were arriving at the hospital in no time. Jackson and Mindy opened the door to a terribly exhausted Allison doing CPR on what looked like a dead body.

"Allison, how long has she been down?"

"She has what looks like a puncture wound on her left side. I think she might have a pneumothorax" She kept pumping, up and down, to the lips and repeat, just like they had taught her when she was a small child.

"Ali, how long?" Jackson insisted as they pulled the gurney to the floor.

"I don't know, just please help" Jackson looked at her little sister, pleading with her with defeated eyes, and he couldn't help but do the best he could for her friend.

They rolled off, leaving her there with blood-covered hands in the middle of the street.

"Allison let's go home and have a shower, and we'll come here right after," Ellie calmly said, moving her sister onto the sidewalk.

"No, I'm not, I can't leave," Her sister was in shock, and Ellie could clearly see the signs, but she wasn't sure how to help her. Allison wasn't going to let her help.

"We need to clean you up, Ali," she said as calmly as possible, but it didn't work.

"I...I need to be here," and with that, she ran into the hospital, rushing into the bathroom.

She stood in front of the mirror and the sink and started crying at the sight of herself as what had just happened flooded into her mind. She started washing her hands, and as the blood started dripping down to the sink, she heard the door open.

The sight of her mother there broke her even more, she couldn't contain herself, and she started bawling as her mother held her tightly in her arms.

"She's alive, Allison. Your brother has just taken her into surgery." she caressed her daughter's hair, trying to calm her down.

"She's going to die just like Parker. I haven't told her so many things, Mom, I have to tell her everything" This was probably one of the first times for Claudia that any of her children opened up to her in that way. Her husband Richard was such a beautiful soul that all their lives, he had been the one to care for their children's problems.

"You'll have all the time in the world, Allison, now go have a shower, change. You are currently suspended while this investigation finishes. You'll be here when she wakes up." After calming down, Allison left but didn't go home.

She went to look for Mindy and was lucky to find her at a nurse's station talking to a patient. She had a shower in the dressing rooms and changed into some of Mindy's spare clothes. Once she had finally calmed down, she went into the waiting room, where many officers were waiting to hear some news. She couldn't help but have flashbacks from Parker's death.

The door opened, and Rachel, Charlie's sister, walked into the waiting room accompanied by two officers walking behind her. Allison didn't see herself capable of talking to her, so she tried walking out discreetly, but she wasn't fast enough. Rachel had seen her and called out her name as she cried.

"Where were you?" She shouted, "You're her partner. Where were you?" She broke apart, and the officers helped her sit on a chair.

Allison couldn't face her, and she ran away into the bathroom to breathe. When she recomposed herself and went back out, finding

Ellie and John talking to Rachel. She was on her way to them to apologize to Rachel when Mindy walked out with a sad face and walked over to them.

"Hello Rachel, I'm Mindy. I'm one of your sister's doctors" She crouched down and held Rachels hands while looking at her with a sad smile. "They're doing everything they can, but you should prepare yourself."

"What? Mindy, no!" Allison's screams made all the attention get put on her. Ellie hugged Rachel tightly as she cried. "That's what you say when a patient is about to die, she, NO MINDY DON'T LET HER DIE!" Mindy held her and walked her further away from all the other police officers that were waiting to hear good news like she was.

This couldn't be happening. Charlie couldn't die without having told her that she also loved her.

"Allison, she lost too much blood. Your brother is trying to do everything he can, I promise, but it is unlikely she'll come out of this. I'm so sorry."

Allison wasn't going to live through this again. Parker's death had been enough for her. She wasn't strong enough. She turned around and headed to the door, but Ellie stopped her before she could leave.

"You don't want to do this. If it's her time and she has to leave, you want to be here, you want to be with her sister who only knows you in this room and is living what you lived through not even a year ago." but Allison didn't listen, it wasn't that she didn't want to. She couldn't.

She brushed her sister off and walked right out of the hospital. She took her phone out and ordered an Uber. She was going to buy junk food and eat it until she felt bad and wanted to throw up. Her Uber arrived in three minutes, and as it left the hospital area, she saw Ellie running out looking for her. She saw how she took out her phone with tears running down her face. Allison's phone started ringing, but she wasn't prepared to hear that she was gone, so she turned her phone off and continued her way.

Ellie

"For fucks sake, Allison," Ellie cursed into her phone as her sister's answering machine was the only thing that answered her. "Allison, she pulled through. Jackson stopped the bleeding. She's going to live. Come back before she wakes up."

But hours went past, and Allison didn't appear. Charlie woke up, and after Rachel had finished with her sister, John and Ellie went in to question her.

"Where is she?" Was the first thing she asked as soon as she saw Ellie.

"They told us you weren't going to make it," she started. But Charlie didn't need her to finish.

"So she left cause she couldn't deal with it."

"Exactly," Ellie answered with a sad smile.

"And I'm guessing she won't answer her phone thinking I'm dead."

"You know her better than me" she tried to laugh, but Charlie's face was really serious.

"We aren't going to be partners anymore, are we?" At that moment, Ellie saw everything as it really was, two young girls who had fallen stupidly in love and just wanted to be together.

"She'll be lucky if she gets her job back, Charlie, but we need to talk about the case if you're up for that?"

"Yeah, but once we're finished, Ellie, please go and get your sister, she… I'm sure all of this is reminding her of Parker."

"I'll go to her apartment as soon as we're finished here, I promise."

Johns questioned her, and after asking some important questions, she had to ask her about the text message.

"Why would you put yourself out that like that after weeks of work?"

"I heard them talking, and I knew I had been made, so the only thing I thought about was texting my partner, who I knew would see the message and understand it at some point. Just as I sent it, they hit me on the head, and I woke up in the room you found me in."

"Wait, what happened to your phone? The one you texted my sister with."

"I, I didn't have it when I woke up."

"So they have Allison's number." Ellie ran as fast as she could, calling the FBI agents she had worked with.

"Oh god," Charlie held her hands to her face crying.

Tom ran out and made a few calls for them to start tracking Allison's phone.

13 I DON'T KNOW WHY YOU SAY GOODBYE

Ellie

Ellie, Claudia, Richard, and Tom all stood in the room where multiple FBI agents talked, trying to figure out their next step.

"So Officer Benzinni was last seen leaving the hospital at twelve hundred hours. She took an Uber home and turned her phone off. The next time her phone was connected was when she reached her apartment building. A few moments later is when we estimate she was abducted." One of the agents started briefing the new agents on the case.

"A note was found beside a puddle of blood on the floor," explained the other agent, which was the one that had been questioning Allison all morning.

Ellie couldn't help but look away as she saw the photograph. The note read:

'No one messes with my business, an eye for an eye. This isn't over yet.'

There was a lot of movement, people talking, and while that was going on, an agent went over to the Benzinni family.

"Commissioner, I have to ask you and your family to stay out of the way and let us work on this one," And even though they left the building, they definitely didn't stop working.

They all met at the house and started planning, they had convinced the FBI to let Tom stay at headquarters in case they needed any extra information about Allison, and he would feed them information that he learned. They also connected via video call with a very distraught Charlie who was trying to remember anything that could be of use.

"I'm pretty sure this whole thing is being conducted by a Rafael Rodríguez." After giving that name to Tom, he called back, telling them he was one of the most wanted on the FBI search list.

They worked and talked for hours on end, and the clock ticking in the Benzinni living room only made everyone feel more nervous.

"I wasn't in that warehouse all the time," Charlie remembered. "I remember the first day I got there, I was taken to this apartment, they had put something in my drink that made me drowsy, but I'm pretty sure it's where Rafael could have maybe been. It was where they took the girls to be validated."

"What do you mean validated?" Richard asked.

"If he didn't like them to work, they didn't come back in the van with us."

"And is there anything you remember about that place?" Ellie was becoming desperate to find something. She couldn't help but feel like it was all her fault.

"The car ride wasn't too long, it couldn't be longer than ten minutes, and it was nighttime, so there weren't many car noises."

"Think about it, Officer Reigns. What noises did you hear?"

Charlie closed her eyes, trying to separate every noise she was hearing that night. She heard her heart beating, people's footsteps, she heard someone's phone ring and pigs. She heard pigs.

"I heard pigs. I remember I was so confused, and I didn't understand why I was hearing pigs, but there were pig noises."

"Pigs?"

"Yeah, pigs, like four-legged, pink dogs with curly tails."

They all looked at each other, thinking.

"There's a farm where I sometimes go with my school children, which is about ten minutes away from where they found you," Rachel's voice made her way into the conversation for the first time.

"Who is that?" Claudia asked.

"My sister, sorry, Commissioner."

"Put her on the phone," Rachel's face appeared on the phone. She looked terribly young. She had a chubby face, brown wavy hair all over the place, and a small smile on her face. "Where is that farm you're talking about?"

"The one I'm thinking about is grey mouse farm on grey mouse road, but Ma'am, there are so many farms around that area, it would be a real coincidence if that was the exact farm."

"Why did you think of that farm when we said pigs?"

"Last time we went there, the pigs were really noisy, the children loved it, but I remember it made my head go crazy."

"It's the best we've got for now." Claudia looked at her husband and her daughter, and they all made their way to the cars. Tom and Ellie went in one while Claudia and Richard went in the other.

"Charlie, Rachel, I need to hang up, but Char, I will let you know as soon as we know something."

They took a while to get to the farm. As they got closer, they drove slowly and made their exit on a nearby street. They walked carefully close enough to see two men with guns guarding the door. They had found the place.

Claudia Benzinni called for backup. Fifteen minutes later, they were raiding the place. Rafael Rodríguez was apprehended, but Allison was nowhere to be found.

ABOUT THE AUTHOR

Mai Roma is a 21 year old aspiring writer, she especially loves writing LGBTQ+ romance stories. She debuted her first novel in December 2020 'LEA' a Spanish written LGBTQ+ drama which sold over 100 copies and has over 100K read on KDP.

She is a loving, talented writer, singer and actress who wants to continue making stories, writing characters and wants to be able to give people an escape from their day to day reality.

She has social media which she will be happy to have you join:

Tiktok: @mairomawriter
Instagram: @soyyomairoma

She will also love hearing all kinds of feedback about this book so she can make the next one better.

Printed in Great Britain
by Amazon